Arianne squeezed her eyes shut. "No, no—it's impossible. I'm just imagining this." She opened her eyes. He was still there. Well, kind of there and not there, all at the same time. He raised a translucent hand to her face, and she felt the breeze of a touch on her cheek. Soft, lingering, a gently electric feeling, a shadow of a touch, a ghost of a touch. A ghost of—

A ghost. Oh my god! Arianne drew back instinctively. He dropped his hand from her face.

"Hey, I thought you'd be kind of glad to see me," he said. "I mean, that's why I'm here."

Oh, Andy! Andy, if only it were true.

"Ari, it is true," he said softly.

She let her eyes roam over his face. The curves and planes she knew so well, the deep-set eyes and full lips, the strong, roman nose, the thick, sandy-colored brows and mop of light brown curls. He had on her favorite navy-blue T, that made his eyes look even bluer, and a pair of faded jean cut-offs. He smiled and she felt a tightness inside her give way.

She smiled back tentatively. "I want this as much as I've ever wanted anything," she said.

enchanted ♥ HEARTS

2

Eternally
Yours

Jennifer Baker

AN AVON FLARE BOOK

AVON BOOKS, INC.
1350 Avenue of the Americas
New York, New York 10019

Copyright © 1999 by Jennifer Baker
Excerpt from *Lost and Found* copyright © 1999 by Mary Cameron Dokey
Published by arrangement with the author
Library of Congress Catalog Card Number: 98-94855
ISBN: 0-380-80073-X
www.avonbooks.com

First Avon Flare Printing: July 1999

AVON FLARE TRADEMARK REG. U.S. PAT. OFF. AND IN OTHER COUNTRIES, MARCA REGISTRADA, HECHO EN U.S.A.

Printed in the U.S.A.

WCD 10 9 8 7 6 5 4 3 2 1

Eternally
Yours

one

*Ari*anne Kessler looked out the car window and watched the familiar landscape roll by her. Low dunes dotted with gray-green scrub brush and fuchsia wild beach plums. A glimpse of the mostly hidden network of dirt fire roads that she and Andy had charted extensively by mountain bike. The row of gray-shingled cottages his uncle rented out in the summer months. Ari's father rounded a curve, and an expanse of ocean appeared behind the dunes, glittering in the morning sun.

Ari sucked in her breath sharply. The beach where *it* happened. She didn't want to see it, but she couldn't look away. Everything so . . . normal, so totally free of any sign, any clue. A few early risers still bundled up in sweatshirts, a jogger, a couple of surfers Ari knew from school. The surfers were just tiny figures out on the water, but she recognized their Jeeps in the beach parking lot.

Dad turned up Cahill Hollow Lane and headed toward the main road, the beach receding in the rearview mirror. A tear slid down Ari's cheek. Now she was really, truly leaving Andy behind.

"Don't cry, L.M." She heard his warm baritone voice deep inside her head. L.M. for Little Mermaid. How many times had she told Andy to quit using that sappy nickname he'd coined for her after she'd aced the hundred meter freestyle at a school swim meet? But now it was comforting to hear it, even if it was just a memento she'd conjured up from the depths of loneliness and longing.

How can I not cry? she answered him silently.

Everyone told her this was a new beginning. A chance to start fresh. To leave the painful memories behind. College! A big university! She'd been waiting so long for this. New places, new faces. A different world from the little town she knew inch by inch, person by person. Arianne's Big Adventure. But Andy was supposed to have been part of the adventure, too.

All last fall they'd poured over college catalogs together. A good theater department for Ari at one school; stately, ivy-covered stone buildings and a movie-perfect campus at another. Good athletic programs? Tuition reduction for state residents? Distance from home? Far but not too far, they'd both agreed.

And when they'd narrowed it down to a chosen few, they'd tested out their new driver's licenses and gone visiting, singing along at top volume to the tunes blasting out of the speakers of Andy's parents' van. Ari had to talk Andy out of choosing a school with his stomach alone, although after one particularly awful tuna casserole at Newton College's main dining hall, she was ready to give at least a few points to any place that could do better.

Interviews. Applications to fill out. "The dude at U. Maine? L.M., he had this big piece of green stuff stuck to one of his front teeth, and I mean, he was perfectly nice and everything, but I was like, I'm leaning toward premed—sports medicine, maybe—and I was in Honors spinach—I mean Spanish . . .''

Ari laughed to herself, then stopped abruptly.

"Honey?" Mom shifted around in the front passenger's seat to make eye contact. People said they looked alike—same oval-shaped face, aquiline nose, and deep-set eyes. But Ari's dark hair had come from Dad's side, and her mouth was fuller than either of theirs. Ari gave her mother a weak smile. Mom smiled back, the bright turn of her mouth unable to conceal the worry in her eyes.

As soon as her mother turned frontwards again, Ari dropped all pretense of a happy expression. The sound of the surf had disappeared altogether, replaced by the hiss of light traffic on Route 20.

Andy and Ari each had received an acceptance letter from the College of New England. They'd toasted their success over dinner at the Anchor Grill. But Andy was never going to make it to college. Never set another freestyle record. Never travel to all those places he talked about. Never get that first real job. He wasn't going to marry and raise a family. And Ari wasn't going to do any of it with him.

Some of her friends had thought she was crazy to want to go away to college with her old high school boyfriend. Her best friend, Loren, insisted that college was for new things—specifically, new boys. Judy Rose was just waiting to go off to school because it was easier than officially dumping Mitchell Caine. Of course, Loren didn't have a boyfriend to dump. And both Loren and Judy admitted that Ari and Andy *were* a perfect couple.

Said it right in this year's yearbook: they were the couple voted Most Likely to Live Happily Ever After.

Yeah, right. In the Ever After, that was. If you believed in those kinds of things.

"Believe it, L.M." Ari sat up, startled. Then she gave her head a shake. That voice inside her mind was just wishful thinking. Besides, what good was the Ever After to her right now? If she was here and Andy was . . . well, wherever. She hated to even think about that.

The cold, hard reality was that Andy wasn't around anymore. Arianne was going to college by herself. Just like Loren and Judy. But it wasn't supposed to have been this way.

two
ℒ

High school graduation. Arianne, in cap and gown, sweeping across the open-air stage set up in the football field. Little sister Zoë, Mom, and Dad cheering from the audience. One by one the senior class collecting their diplomas. Andy flashing a thumbs-up sign as he crosses the stage. Principal Plung working his way through the alphabet: Jody Wilkens, Donald Wurt, Lillian Yee . . . and finally, wild-haired wild man Steven Zorn raising his fist high. Everyone on his or her feet. Tasseled caps thrown in the air and raining back down. Ari in Andy's arms, her feet off the ground as he spins her around.

The party after. Ari in a long, elegant gown, jet-black like her hair, which is swept up in a French twist. Andy in his rented tux. Tall, handsome, blue eyes sparkling, light brown curls just starting to be streaked blond by the early-summer sun. He pins a purple-and-white orchid onto Ari's dress. She can smell its perfume.

A live band on the deck of the Holiday Inn. Dancing under the stars. A huge buffet. A bottle of champagne. The chaperons look the other way. They were high school graduates once, too. Andy going over to talk to the band. Asking them to play his and Ari's song. The first chords of "If You Feel" rising up into the night. Ari melting into Andy's arms. His strong, graceful movements, the sheer happiness as they dance together.

The parties after the party. Everyone's going over to Mitchell's. Then a smaller group at Jody's. The music gets mellower. People are chilling. Stevie Zorn in an old, broken-in armchair, out like a light. Let him sleep if off.

Breakfast at the twenty-four-hour diner, out by the thruway. Ari not realizing how hungry she is. She and Andy split bacon and eggs and the banana-walnut pancakes. Andy makes a heart in strawberry jelly on a piece of toast and gives it to her. Everyone at the table groans and laughs. Loren makes a gag-me face. "Okay, so I'm a fool for love," Andy says lightly.

They get a second wind. All of a sudden, no one's tired anymore. Can they make it back to the beach by sunrise? They pile into their cars and caravan home. Horns honking. Headlights flashing like strobes. Make way for the graduates! They get to the beach just as the horizon is glowing bright pink.

"Let's swim out and meet the sun!" Ari says to Andy, tugging at his hand. They're running down the dunes, laughing, shedding down to their underthings and leaving their dress-up clothes crumpled on the sand. The waves are pounding the shore. Ari races right into the water and dives under the first big curl. The water is still bracing this time of year. She swims out with powerful strokes, glancing back once to see Andy pulling near her.

They cut through the cold salt water like pros. Quickly, they leave the beach behind. Ari feels like they really could swim out to meet the sun. And there it is—the fiery top popping up out of the water on the horizon! It's going to be a beautiful day.

But suddenly, they're getting closer to meeting the sun than they'd planned. Ari looks back at the shoreline, and it's very far away. Their friends on the beach are so small she can barely see them. She feels the dangerous pull of the ocean carrying her swiftly out to sea. She feels a beat of fear. She waves her arms to get Andy's attention, treading hard with her legs. She points back to land. They need to turn around. But even as she's signaling frantically, the riptide is dragging her farther out. Farther and farther.

Arianne turns around and pulls her arms through the water with all her might. But she makes no progress. She's battling just to stay in place. Arm over arm, legs fluttering as fast as she can move them. Her heart is racing out of control. Her muscles burn as she pulls her arms through the vicious current. Not even at her most important swim meet has she swum this hard.

Frantically, she looks around for Andy. He's pointing, shouting. "Across the current. Cross it, Ari!"

Of course! Panicking, she'd forgotten what she has always known. You swim out of the riptide, parallel to the shore. Once you're free of it, you can start swimming in.

She changes direction. She's gasping for breath. Fear, exhaustion, the numbing cold of the water. She can't feel her hands or feet. She's trying to swim out of the ocean's deadly grip, but her arms and legs are growing weak. She picks up her head and sees that Andy is still swimming strong and straight, making his way out of the dangerous tide. She tries to call to him, but her words are carried off on the wind. The gap between them widens.

Ari lets her arms and legs hang down in the energy-conserving float she learned years ago in junior life-saving. Her face is in the water and she lifts it only to take a breath. She needs to gather a bit of her strength. But the fear pumping through her body is draining her, and she can feel the riptide carrying her like a piece of driftwood.

Suddenly, Andy is swimming back to her. His arm goes around her in a cross-chest carry. Her body against his, she can feel his heart beating overtime. He tows her through the water, and his muscles are taut with exertion.

Finally, the pull of the riptide subsides. Andy starts swimming them both toward shore. "We're okay now, Ari. We're okay. Do you think you can make it in on your own?"

Ari eases out of his hold and begins stroking. Weakly, now, but the beach is getting closer. Her fear starts to lose its grasp. She can see her friends waiting for them on the sand. She turns over on her back and changes her stroke. And suddenly, a huge wave is crashing down on her face. She takes in a mouthful of water as she's pulled under. She fights her way up, spitting salt water and gasping for air.

But she has been rolled right back into the riptide. She screams for help, flailing her arms. Andy? She doesn't see him anywhere. Then his head pops up a few yards away. But a moment later it's gone.

Now their friends have caught sight of them. Jody Wilkens is charging into the waves. A veteran life-guard at Cahill Hollow Beach, in no time he's got Ari and is pulling her in. She surrenders herself to him, and he carries her out of the water and lays her down on the sand.

And Andy? "Where's Andy?" Ari hears Jody asking. She sits bolt upright and scans the water. Then the beach. The water again.

She's on her feet. "Andy! Oh, my god, Andy!" And all her friends are racing to the water's edge. Andy! Andy!

But all they see is the rising and falling of the ocean, the gleaming surface of the water, the white crash of foam as the waves hit. Andy is gone.

Andy uses his last bit of strength to fight his way up to the surface and take a gasp of air. Arianne! He spots her just as Jody Wilkens is getting her in his grip. He breathes a sigh of relief and lets himself go limp, just as another wave breaks over his head. And he's going down again, down, down, and he doesn't have force to fight it anymore. His lungs are burning, about to burst. He's holding out, holding . . . and then he can't. He takes a huge, watery breath. He's flooded with a pleasant, dizzy feeling. He's light, his body relaxing. He's giving in. . . .

Ari on the shore, screaming Andy's name. Loren holding her, telling her they're going to get him, wrapping her in someone's too-big suit jacket. Jody diving back into the water. Ari hearing the terror in her own voice. "Andy! Oh, please, Andy!"

The wait. Oh, where are they? Are they ever going to come out?

And then, Jody dragging Andy out. But he's limp. Motionless. His body being laid down on the sand. The vain efforts to bring him back to life. Jody's hands on Andy's heart. One, two, three, push. One, two, three. Jody's mouth on Andy's mouth, trying to breath his own life into his friend's body. The frenzied voices of everyone watching.

And worst of all, the dead quiet that follows. Jody standing up, stepping back, shaking his head. There's nothing else that he can do. Two words: "He's gone."

Andy is lifting high above the water, caressed by a brilliant, shimmering light. The terror of his battle with the ocean has vanished completely. He's floating in a peaceful silence. Calm. A tremendous weight has been lifted from him. He's filled with a powerful sense of well-being, of love, of belonging. Belonging to what? He's not sure, yet, but there's something familiar about the way he feels. As if he's arriving in a place he has been before. No tension. No worry. No boundaries. He's going home.

Down below, his body lies on the sand. It's as if he has shed it, like a jacket he didn't need anymore. He watches Jody's frightened efforts to save his life. Arianne's hollow, disbelieving gaze. Ari. His Little Mermaid. Now she's calling out to him in desperation.

It takes all his focus to try to call back. To turn away from the joy and radiant light. He forms her name, but she can't hear his words. Already, they're worlds apart. She can't hear him, can't see him. He's lighter, being lifted higher, farther away . . .

three

That summer, on the beach where he'd died, Arianne heard his voice in her head for the first time. It was a cloudy, late afternoon, and a cool breeze was coming off the water. Ari walked along the shoreline until she reached an empty stretch of sand. She sat down, drew up her knees, and wrapped her arms around them. She knew everyone thought she was crazy, spending hours alone on this beach, but it was the last place she and Andy had been together, and somehow, being there made her feel closer to him.

She'd just gotten off working the brunch shift at Elaine's. A morning rain shower had brought the vacationers in by droves, and her pockets were stuffed with bills and coins. A chorus of orders echoed in her mind. Eggs Florentine and a decaf cappuccino. Two tropical chicken salad sandwiches, one on white, one on whole wheat . . .

"Oh, and can you leave off the grapes on mine?" she heard Andy say. "And the mayo, too."

Andy? Ari whipped her head around, but of course she was alone.

"In fact, don't put the chicken on that, either. Just the celery pieces and pineapple. And don't overtoast the bread."

11

Okay, Andy wasn't there, but it was just like something he'd say when she'd come home railing about a picky customer. She laughed to herself.

"There's that smile. That's what I was looking for." Andy's voice again! It really was!

Except that it couldn't be, and Ari knew it. It was only the product of her own wishful imagination.

Yet, Andy's voice was so real Ari found herself answering out loud. "Oh, Andy, how can I smile when you're not with me? How can I smile when there's never, ever going to be a chance for 'happily ever after'?" She was surprised by how the tone of her own words shifted from sadness to anger, tumbling out with a hardness she hadn't expected.

Well, maybe she *was* angry. Angry, sad, frightened. If the weeks immediately following the accident had been bad, the ones she was living now were even worse. At first, Ari had been too filled with shock to feel the aching hole in her life. The accident and its aftermath had consumed her. The police reports. The funeral. The hours with friends and family, sharing memories and stories of Andy.

It was when life went back to normal—at least for Loren and Judy and the rest of the gang—that the misery of losing Andy really set in. It hurt to see people going about their everyday business—shopping, working, hanging out—exactly, completely, totally the way they always had. It didn't make sense that every muscle in Arianne's body was tight with tragedy, her world abruptly changed, yet around her nothing was different at all. People still moaning about the price of a grilled cheese at Elaine's, still laughing about some joke on last night's episode of *Friends*. It made her feel separate from everyone around her, in a place apart, as if she had died in that swimming accident, too. Lots of days she wished she had.

Especially hard were all those firsts. First time driving by the rambling white house where he'd lived. First time picking up a quart of milk in the deli where he'd worked after school. First time going out with the gang without him. None of them seemed quite sure how to deal with Ari. Be extra nice to her and risk making her feel singled out? Pretend everything was fine and just cruise along, imitating normal? And then there'd been the first time she'd heard "If You Feel" on the radio. She'd turned it right off. It had just been too painful.

"You mean, you think they should retire the song like a basketball jersey, L.M.?"

And suddenly, there she was, on the beach, laughing again. And then laughing and crying at the same time, because it felt as if Andy were so near and they had shared so many incredible times. Her face was wet and her body was shaking, and there was no one around to see, so she just let it all out. When her sobs quieted she felt better. She'd needed the release.

After that, she'd started going to the beach often. Instead of going out with Loren and the others. Ari knew she just made them too uncomfortable, anyway. She'd stare out at the sea. Remember the feel of Andy's hand in hers as they'd run down the dunes that last time, the sound of their laughter as they'd hit the cold water, the freedom in swimming together, just the two of them. And then she'd imagine that they'd simply turned around when they'd swum far enough. That they'd easily, naturally made their way back to shore. She'd picture Andy coming out of the water, the way he had of shaking the excess water off his wet curls. And the harder she pictured a happier ending, the easier it was to hear his voice.

"Hey, check out that cloud. Remember that chem sub we had when Ms. Clarkson was on maternity leave? The one with that ski jump for a nose? Looks like her profile, don't you think?" he might say. Or maybe, more simply, "Looks like it's gonna pour, L.M. Better get home before you get soaked."

Mom said the whole thing with Andy would get less sharp and painful with time. That one day she'd realize the memories were less raw around the edges. That a moment would go by when she'd forget to think about him. Forget? Andy? The sound of his voice? Never. Arianne didn't want to and she wouldn't. She was going to carry him with her forever.

four
D

So, here we are. Eakens Hall, *Arianne thought, half* to herself, half to some comforting, conjured-up idea of Andy. *Not my first choice for a dorm, but the location's good.* First choice had been a divided double in one of the newer dorms. The new buildings were farther away from the center of campus, and there was a wall between your section of the room and your roommate's, so you had a little more privacy than in an open double. But Eakens was right on North Quad, a two-minute walk from most of the main buildings, and directly across from the brand-new, state-of-the-art gym. Besides, the tiny half rooms in the divided doubles were a lot like walk-in closets. The Eakens rooms offered a little more space.

"And anyway, you're not coming to college for privacy," Andy's voice said. She knew that's what he would have told her, had he been right beside her in the backseat. "I mean, look at all the new folks around here, right?"

Ari looked out the car window as Dad pulled into the North Quad parking lot, across from her dorm. A bunch of kids were tossing a Frisbee out on the lawn. Two girls sat under a big tree, talking animatedly. A tall, thin guy with dark curls and an interesting face came out of the Eakens main entrance toting his guitar.

Ari felt a trill of excitement as she got out of the car. Despite being here without Andy. And anyway, he was right about the new folks. Or would have been right if he'd really been there, talking to her.

She helped Mom and Dad pull her boxes and duffel bags out of the trunk, and they lugged them across the street and down the narrow walkway to the dorm. Ahead of them, a tall blonde and her equally tall and blonde mother were trying to get through the front door with a dolly piled almost ceiling-high with trunks and suitcases, boxes and bags. Next to the dolly stood a long rack of hanging clothes.

"Better hope she's not your roommate, or you're going to be sleeping out in the hall once she gets finished putting away all her stuff," Ari heard Andy say. He gave her a light swat on the arm for emphasis. Okay, so it was a sudden gusty breeze on her arm. She could dream, couldn't she? She let out a long sigh.

Her mother fixed her with a worried look. "Honey, just try to be in the here and now for a few minutes. Be here with us. It'll help, I know it, even though you might not think so." She put her hand on Ari's arm—right where Ari had imagined Andy's touch.

Ari knew exactly what her mother meant to say: Be here among the living. She shook her mother's hand away. She *was* here. She was taking in everything. The grassy stretches of campus, the mix of old, ivy-covered stone buildings and newer brick ones, the students hanging out in the sun or just getting out of cars, the gleaming metal-and-glass gymnasium, all angles and planes, where she'd be swimming if she made the team this semester. So, she was incorporating Andy's point of view, too. Kind of doing the looking for both of them. She hoped Mom and Dad weren't planning on sticking around too long. She wanted to check out her new home without them telling her how to do it.

But she simply shrugged. "I'll be fine, Mom. Promise."

"She will, Mrs. Kessler, um, Sylvia." Just before his death, Andy had started calling Ari's mother by her first name, and he hadn't gotten entirely used to it. "I'm going to make sure of it."

Alone! Finally!

Arianne plunked down on her new bed. Her roommate had apparently beat her to school, though the only sign of her was her unpacked luggage, haphazardly splayed on the bare floor. A huge duffel bag, a few mismatched suitcases, and an impressive assortment of smaller bags and totes—a straw beach basket overflowing with clothes, some kind of South American–looking knapsack woven in bright colors, a backpack, a number of paper shopping bags. All Ari knew from the room assignment form she'd gotten in the mail several weeks earlier was that her roommate's name was Wendy and she was from San Diego, in Southern California. Ari hoped they were going to get along.

The room itself was pretty standard fare. Two single beds on metal springs. Ari's squeaked slightly as she shifted around on it. Two plain wooden desks and two desk chairs. Two bulky, ugly chests of drawers, a mirror above one of them. One closet, empty for now. An ample set of bookshelves. The bedspreads and curtains were a muddy orange-and-brown swirling pattern. The place definitely needed some personal touches.

But for now, Ari lay back and just enjoyed the moment of solitude. All summer, Mom and Dad, and even Zoë, had been hovering around, fretting about her. Loren came by almost every day at the end of Ari's shift at Elaine's, even though Ari had more or less stopped going out with her friends after work. But now she could feel however she wanted to feel, think about Andy as much as she wanted, without having to put on a brave face for anyone.

She got up and looked around for her panda knapsack in the pile of still-packed stuff. Inside, she'd squirreled away a few prize possessions: a pair of earrings Andy had given her for her last birthday—tiny silver hands holding long, amber, teardrop-shaped stones; a photo of Andy and her before the graduation party; and most important of all, a white T-shirt of Andy's she'd borrowed after spilling a glass of lemonade on herself at his house. The shirt still smelled faintly of him.

Ari put it to her nose and breathed in deeply. When she breathed out, tears were running down her cheeks. She heaved noisily. Her body shook. She threw herself facedown on the bed and let her misery pour out.

"Hey, hey, L.M." She heard his voice and felt his breezy touch again, caressing her arms, stroking her hair. If she didn't know better . . .

She sat up. And let out a scream of sheer terror. Andy was sitting right next to her on the bed. Or a kind of shimmery, not entirely solid version of Andy. As if he was made from the contours of light and shadow, not of flesh and blood and bone. Arianne's heart beat a drumroll of fear.

"Wait, don't be scared," he said. "It's just me."

Arianne squeezed her eyes shut. "No, no—it's impossible. I'm just imagining this." She opened her eyes. He was still there. Well, kind of there and not there, all at the same time. He raised a translucent hand to her face, and she felt the breeze of a touch on her cheek. Soft, lingering, a gently electric feeling, a shadow of a touch, a ghost of a touch. A ghost of—

A ghost! Oh my god! Arianne drew back instinctively. He dropped his hand from her face.

"Hey, I thought you'd be kind of glad to see me," he said. "I mean, that's why I'm here."

Oh, Andy! Andy, if only it were true.

"Ari, it is true," he said softly.

She let her eyes roam over his face. The curves and planes she knew so well, the deep-set eyes and full lips, the strong roman nose, the thick sandy-colored brows and mop of light brown curls. He had on her favorite navy-blue T that made his eyes look even bluer, and a pair of faded jean cutoffs. He smiled, and she felt a tightness inside her give way.

She smiled back tentatively. "I want this as much as I've ever wanted anything," she said. "But you can't be sitting here, Andy. It's just impossible."

He laughed. "What does it look like to you, L.M.?"

"Like you're sitting here. And would you stop calling me L.M.?"

"Nope," Andy said.

Ari couldn't help but laugh. It just felt so right, so familiar to her. If this was a vision, she never wanted it to end. "That *was* you talking to me all summer!"

"Well, you knew it, didn't you?"

"Yeah, I did," said Ari. And as she said it, she knew it was true. She'd felt Andy with her, no doubt

19

about it. During the long walks on the beach where she'd talked to him and he'd answered. When she'd felt like she was hitting rock bottom and he'd told her a joke and suddenly she was laughing. "But I was afraid to believe it, Andy. You know how crazy this seems?"

Andy shrugged. "How could I leave you, Ari? You needed me. I could feel it. And the more you needed me, the stronger your thoughts of me, the more I was able to . . . Well, you see what I'm saying."

"I'm starting to," Ari said, the joy creeping into her voice. Andy! Here with her again! Here with her like always! And if he was a ghost, well, she'd take him whatever way she could.

She threw her arms around him. It felt more like a kind of energy than the presence of a solid body—a tingle of electricity or current of air or water. She could touch him and put her hand right through him at the same time. But it was Andy, and they were together!

She ran her fingertips over his face, feeling the boundaries of the current where she'd once followed the outline of his features. The contours were the very same ones she'd traced so many times. Oh, this was Andy! Ari felt herself brimming with happiness. She was crying again, but this time there was no sorrow in her tears.

She touched his lips with her fingers. He kissed them, a light, electric breeze. He cupped her face in his hands. She turned her mouth up to his, and she could feel herself trembling. Their lips met in a potent charge of magnetism. She could feel the current flowing between them. It was unlike any kiss she'd ever experienced, pure friction and intensity and power, while as light and delicate as air. Totally other-worldly.

"Andy," she sighed, and let him wrap her in his electric caress. She kissed him again and again.

And suddenly she heard the doorknob rattle. She jumped away from Andy just as the door was pulled open. A petite, pretty redhead in baggy jeans, sandals, and a purple-and-yellow Lakers T-shirt took a step into the room.

Ari could feel herself blushing furiously. Caught! But the girl just smiled. "Oh, hey! Cool, you finally got here!" She came toward Ari with her hand outstretched.

Ari glanced at Andy. He raised his shoulders and gave her a lopsided smile, but he was very faint, almost invisible. She could see right through him to the telephone on the wall near the door.

Wendy took Ari's hand and started to shake it. Then, changing her mind, she threw her arms around Ari, impulsively turning the formal gesture into a friendlier one. "Hey, I mean, we're going to be living in the same room. Let's not be strangers," she said with a giggle, sitting right down in the exact spot where Andy already sat. Wendy couldn't see him at all!

Andy shifted over, so that Wendy was between him and Ari. He looked around Wendy and arched an eyebrow at Ari.

Ari's head spun. She felt overwhelmed. "Um, uh, nice to meet you, Wendy," she managed to say.

"Likewise, Arianne. That's a cool name. I always wished my parents had named me something more unusual, you know? I had a few months in high school where I wanted people to call me Cinnamon. Pretty dumb, huh?"

Andy leaned forward so Ari could see him. "Cinnamon?" he said. "Well, she *is* from California."

Wendy didn't hear a thing. Ari shot Andy a look that said "Behave." "I think Wendy's a pretty name," she said. "And you can call me Ari."

"Sure," Wendy said easily. "Hey, how was your trip? Folks gone already? I swear, I thought my mom was going to move in."

Ari laughed. "I know what you mean." Wendy seemed nice. "I really had to work on mine to get them to hit the road."

"The old separation anxiety," Wendy commented. "Well, but here we are, and now it's just us. Isn't it great?"

Ari looked at Andy. Then at Wendy. "Uh, yeah, really great. Just us." She looked back at Andy.

He smiled and shrugged, then gave a little wave. "Later," he mouthed, and suddenly he was gone.

Arianne felt a jolt of panic. "No! Wait, Andy . . ." Her words slipped right out.

"Andy?" Wendy followed Ari's gaze into thin air. "Ari, are you okay?" she asked, her voice a mixture of concern and wariness. "Who's Andy?"

Arianne's face grew hot with embarrassment. "Oh, never mind. I'm . . . I'm really sorry. I don't know what got into me . . ."

Wendy shifted away from Ari. Ari could see that Wendy was afraid she had gotten a nutcase for a roommate.

"Look, Wendy . . . Please don't think I'm crazy. Andy's my boyfriend. I mean, was my boyfriend. He died. Right after graduation. Sometimes . . . well, sometimes . . ." Her words trailed off. Sometimes what? Sometimes I hear him? Sometimes I talk to him? Sometimes he pops right in and starts kissing me?

If it hadn't just happened, Ari would think that last part sounded totally nuts, too. She looked to the spot where Andy had just been. Maybe it *was* nuts. Maybe she missed Andy so badly she was losing it. Hearing voices. Seeing things. The joy she'd felt just a few moments before was replaced by a trill of fear. "I don't know what to think," she whispered.

Wendy moved back toward her and gave her shoulder a little squeeze. "It must be really awful for you. I'm really sorry. Look, if there's anything I can do . . . if you need to talk about it or something . . . well, you can talk to me, okay?"

Ari nodded, her head filled with confusion. Andy had died. Yet that kiss had been real.

Andy was so glad to see Ari's smile again. She'd been so sad all summer it had broken his heart. Now he floated above the CNE campus, idly watching the new students arrive and thinking of the sparkle in Ari's brown eyes.

He hadn't told her how hard it had been to stay. How hard it continued to be. The silvery, shimmery light that had embraced him after the accident, the warmth and sense of peace, were just about irresistible. It was like the first day of spring after a hard winter, the softness of the air on blissfully bare skin, the sweet hint of honeysuckle, day-to-day concerns just lifting away. No hurry, no worries, nothing that couldn't wait till tomorrow. The best first day of vacation you could possibly imagine, times about a zillion.

Andy could feel it even now. Like jubilant music that resonated through every part of his soul. And as he let it fill him, the campus below him began to slip away.

But through the joy, a note of unhappiness. Ari's unhappiness. Andy pulled himself back to her by sheer force of will, the way he might have summoned up some impossible reserve for the final few strokes of a winning race, even though he'd already given it everything he had. He could sense her calling him, sense her need, and he focused on it as if it were a finish line.

He scanned the campus from all angles at once, simultaneously looking inside the buildings and out. He zeroed in on Ari's misery, pulling himself toward it until he spotted her in her new room—alone again. She held their graduation picture in her hand. Andy pushed away the golden feeling of bliss and tapped into the strength of Arianne's emotions. After the kiss they'd shared, he was more in tune with them than ever. He sensed her confusion, her doubt. He heard her call out to him, and her call was like his anchor in her world. He gathered his energy to join her.

Very faintly, he felt a thought. Outside him, inside, he couldn't say. *Do what you have to, but don't lose your way.*

"*You're back!*" *Ari didn't waste a second this time.* "Quick, what was I wearing the first day of eleventh grade?"

"How could I forget the first time I saw you? A pair of blue-and-green boxer shorts and a Warren High girls' soccer T-shirt. Those Airwalk sports sandals. And your hair flowing and long."

"What was the name of Mrs. Peterson's pet gerbil?"

"You mean the one that got loose and came to an unfortunate end? Sweet Pea. Should have been Stinky, by the time they found him." Ari laughed. Andy was right about that one. This was absolutely, definitely the Andy she knew and loved.

But wait! What was she thinking? If she was looking for confirmation that he was really here, this wasn't it. He wasn't telling her anything she didn't already know. If Andy was a vision she was calling up in her mind, then she could be calling up his answers, too. Not exactly the proof positive she'd been looking for. She reigned in her elation and gave a sigh.

Andy seemed to know what she was thinking. "Okay, how about something you *don't* know, then? Can you see out the window from here? The one over on Wendy's side?"

Ari craned her neck, but only a part of a tree was visible. "Just a few branches and some leaves," she said. "Looks like a maple."

"Well, there's this guy down there with a really weird hat," Andy said. "Looks like the one from *The Cat in the Hat*, or something."

Ari went over and looked out the window. Her pulse sped up as she saw the yard-high hat in red-and-white stripes, its owner just sitting under a tree checking things out. She looked back at Andy and he grinned. "Whoa! How'd you do that?"

Andy shrugged. "I just kind of went there. I mean, I was still here, too."

"You were? I mean, you did? I mean, you can do that?" Ari felt a stirring of wonder.

"And for an encore, why don't you try looking out in the hall?" he suggested. "The one with all the luggage is heading for the room a couple of doors down."

Ari opened her door and peered out. Sure enough, the tall blonde was going into the second-to-last room on the same side of the hall! Ari gasped. She felt her earlier exuberance returning. Andy was with her. He really, truly was!

As she turned back, she caught sight of someone else coming down the hall from the other side. Wendy was leaving the bathroom and heading her way. Ari gave a little wave and pulled her head back into the room.

"She's coming back! Wendy's coming back!" she told Andy.

Andy didn't move a muscle. "Whoa, it's okay, L.M. She doesn't know I'm here, anyway."

"Just don't go disappearing like you did before," Arianne pleaded. "I need to get used to the idea that you're really around. When you left before I thought I was going crazy."

Andy came over and kissed her cheek. There it was again, that electric pleasure. "Don't worry, Ari, it's really me."

And then Wendy stepped through the door and there were three of them in the room again. Ari shifted uncomfortably and went over and sat back down on her bed. Wendy gave a hesitant smile and stuffed her hands in the front pockets of her oversized jeans. "So . . ." she said.

Neither girl was sure what was next. While Andy had been out of the room, they'd already swapped all the basic information. Where are you from? What are you into? What's your family like? Why did you choose CNE?

They figured out that they'd probably been paired for their interest in theater. Wendy was an actress and also a pretty serious dancer. Or maybe it was their hometowns, which were both on the beach. Although Wendy's home strip was the Pacific rather than the Atlantic. And her big town saw plenty of action all warm and sunny year long, whereas Ari counted on the long off-season lull for some peace and small-town quiet.

Plus, Wendy had purposely chosen a school as far away from home as possible. Her parents were in the middle of a messy divorce, she'd told Ari, and she wanted to put as much distance between her and ground zero as she could.

"Nothing like eternal love," Wendy had said, with equal parts bitterness and sadness.

Now, as Andy sat down beside Ari, she thought herself incredibly lucky. If this wasn't eternal love, what was? She snuggled next to Andy and felt his electricity. She couldn't help smiling from a place deep inside.

"Feeling better?" Wendy observed. She pulled out her desk chair and took a seat.

"Yeah, thanks," Ari said simply.

"Oh, hey, I forgot to tell you. There's an Eakens picnic lunch in an hour. Out on the quad, for all of us who've arrived for orientation, so we can start getting to know one another."

Arianne looked over at Andy. "Oh. I, um, you know, I still have all this unpacking to do." Of course, Wendy had plenty of it to do herself.

Wendy furrowed her forehead. "So do it later. There's no one around anymore to tell you to clean your room or anything. I mean, unless you're one of those real Felix Unger kind of people. Hold on. Don't tell me you like to make your bed with hospital corners?"

Ari could hear Andy laughing along with her. "As if," he mumbled under his breath.

"No, I'm not a neat freak," Ari answered Wendy with a giggle.

"Well, that's probably good. Otherwise, I was going to have to think maybe they made a mistake putting us together. So, okay, then how about the picnic?" Wendy asked.

Ari felt Andy give her side a little tickle. "Go," he encouraged.

Ari felt a wave of resistance. She'd missed him too long to just walk away. And she wondered if he'd still be waiting for her when she got back. "But . . ."

"But what?" Wendy asked.

"She's right," Andy said. "First day of college and all that. Freshman orientation week. I mean, don't you want to see who's in your dorm? Who you're going to be living with for the entire year? I'm curious about it myself, actually. So how about if I come with you, okay?"

Ari smiled. Now that was a good solution. Have her cake and eat it, too. "Okay," she said. "Sure, I'll go."

"Great!" Wendy replied.

"Great!" Andy echoed.

Ari gave an incredulous laugh. This was totally weird. Totally out there. But in a strange way, it was just how it was supposed to be. First day of CNE. And here was Andy by her side. Exactly as they'd planned it.

Okay, not exactly. But for the first time in months, Arianne felt happy.

The *Cat in the Hat* guy was there. And the luggage girl. And the guy she'd seen with his guitar when she and her parents were just pulling in. And several dozen other new students, milling around the Eakens end of the North Quad, eating barbecued wings and corn and potato salad. There was sweet, ripe watermelon for dessert.

Ari had the watermelon first. She bit into a piece and the juice ran down her chin. "Mmm." It was the first time she'd noticed the taste of anything all summer. It hit the spot, especially in the hot sun.

"Andy, you've gotta have a bite of this," she said softly. She looked up at him as they stood in a shady spot under a tree. She picked up the wedge of water-melon and began to offer it to him. Abruptly, she put it back on the paper plate. She didn't suppose Andy needed to eat any longer. He didn't look overly warm, either. While Ari felt her cheeks flush with heat, her forehead moist, not a single, damp stray curl stuck to Andy's brow. His handsome face looked cool and col-lected.

He turned his light-shadow palms up, as if to say "What can you do?"

On the other side of Ari, someone said, "Excuse me?"

Ari whirled around to face the Cat in the Hat. "Did I hear you saying something?" he wanted to know.

"Oh." Ari was going to have to start being more careful. "I was just thinking this watermelon is so delicious."

"Food service can't do much to ruin a watermelon, huh?" the boy said. "Secret to institutional dining. Eat low on the food chain. Or eat out. I've scoped out the local Taco Time already."

Ari laughed. "Taco Time? Talk about low on the food chain. And by the way, I like the hat."

The boy doffed it quickly, then returned it to his head. "Thank you. I'm Larry," he introduced him-self.

"And these are Thing One and Thing Two." Ari was startled at the sound of Andy's voice in her ear. But of course he was still behind her, close. She man-aged to give Larry's hand a subtle squeeze.

Wendy came over, her plate loaded with potato salad and two pieces of corn. "Ah, the vegetarian plate," Larry observed. "Health reasons, or to protect our fine, furry friends?" He made a rodent face and brought his hands up to his chin.

Looked like they had found the class clown.

Wendy laughed. "Little bit of both. Looks like you're a cat lover, yourself."

As Ari made the introductions, they were joined by Larry's roommate, Bill. "I guess you were right. That hat is a conversation starter," he said to Larry.

"Oh, you mean it's not my effervescent personality?" Larry cracked.

"Effervescent. Extra credit word," Bill tossed back. "So, where are you ladies from?"

That was the question it always got down to—where you'd grown up and gone to high school. By the time Ari had worked her way through dinner and another two pieces of watermelon, she knew the names of the towns everyone called home. And in what wing and on what floor of Eakens they were living. And a number of people's possible majors, as well. Even though she didn't remember half of the names.

The luggage girl was Leslie from New York. Well, a town a half hour outside of New York. She managed the amazing feat of eating a slice of watermelon without getting a drop on her top-to-toe white outfit. Andy thought someone needed to accidentally on purpose step on one of her perfectly white tennis shoes. "And obviously, I can't do the trick," he'd added.

Shelly was Ari's and Wendy's across-the-hall neighbor. She was from Boston, and her roommate hadn't arrived yet. She had a broad Massachusetts accent and an even broader smile. Andy thought she seemed nice, even though she'd sat right on top of him on the grass.

But Ari was going to have to get used to that, too. Someone would put her hand through Andy or put his plate in Andy's lap, or walk right through him. Andy would simply disappear and turn up somewhere else. Mostly in the shadier spots, Ari noticed. In the bright sunlight, he seemed to fade almost to invisible. Of course, she was the only one who seemed to notice him at all.

As she tossed out her plate and helped herself to another cup of punch, she looked around for him. There he was, standing a distance away from the crowd, under the big, leafy tree she could see from the dorm room window. He was listening to the guitar player, who sat cross-legged, playing softly.

Arianne went over and listened along. The boy's fingers picked out a melody and a harmony at the same time. A folksy-bluesy tune.

"He's good," Andy commented, and Ari nodded.

The boy looked up, smiled, picked out a few more notes, and stopped playing. "Hi," he said.

"Hi," Ari answered. "Hey, don't let us—me— stop you. It sounds really nice."

"Thanks," the boy said. "I was working on a new song. Called 'The Orientation Rag'."

"Really? Can I hear it?" Ari asked.

The boy strummed a few notes. "It's not finished or anything, but here's the chorus." He led in with a riff of fancy picking. Then a simple chord and he began singing. "What's your name? Where're you from? And what did you get on your SATs? We're doin' . . . doin' the Orientation Rag. What's your major? Who's your roommate? And what did you get on your SATs? Yup, doin' . . . doin' the Orientation Rag . . ." The tune was lyrical and melodic—a perfect counterpoint to the mundane words.

Arianne burst out laughing.

"Pretty silly, huh?" The boy laughed along. He had a warm smile that creased his thin, angled face and lit up his brown eyes.

"Perfect," Ari countered. "I mean, silly *and* perfect. That's exactly what we've all been saying to each other. Well, except that no one has asked me about my SATs."

"But they want to," the boy said. "They just don't know you well enough yet."

Ari giggled. There might be a grain of truth to that.

"So . . ." the boy said, "what *is* your name? Where're you from? And what did you get—No! Wait! I've got a better idea. Don't tell me any of that. None of it at all. Just tell me . . . um, okay—what's your favorite time of day?"

His question was a breath of fresh air. Not that Ari wasn't having fun getting to know her new neighbors and schoolmates. In fact, she was as curious as anyone to find out where everyone had grown up. One girl she'd met had come all the way from France—Corinne or Carenne, she'd said her name was—and one of the guys from the quad at the end of Ari's hall was from Korea by way of Boston.

But none of them had come even close to asking about her favorite time of day. "Sunset," she answered without hesitation. "The way the light and colors keep changing, that feeling of mellowing out . . . And what about you? What's your favorite part of the day?"

"I love a beautiful sunset," the boy agreed. "But I get a real rush when the sun's just coming up. Whole day ahead of you, and anything could happen. All the possibilities, you know? 'Course, I'm not usually up that early in the morning. But when I am . . . You ever get up to watch the sun rise?"

Ari had a flash of the last time she'd seen the sun come up. The fiery ball popping out of the ocean— and the deadly scene that came afterward. Suddenly, she was choked by fear. She whipped her head around and realized that Andy was no longer with her. She scanned the mingling crowd of new faces. No glimmering sign of him. Her heart pounded.

And then she spotted him wandering away from the picnic, barely visible in the sunlight, his legs and feet fading to invisible so that he appeared to be hovering above the grass. "Um, would you excuse me for a minute?" Ari asked hurriedly. She was terrified that Andy was about to disappear. Without waiting for the boy's answer, she rushed off.

"Okay, so now I know you aren't a morning person," she heard him calling after her.

Ari caught up with Andy and grabbed his hand. She felt that charged tingle and her fear subsided. "Hey, where are you running off to?" she asked.

Andy shrugged. "Just taking a breather from the getting-to-know-you crowd. Besides, you seemed like you were doing fine on your own with what's-his-name over there."

Arianne felt a touch of annoyance. It had been Andy's idea to come to this picnic. "I don't know what his name is," she said, a bit too sharply.

"Hey, mellow, L.M. Like I said, I just needed a break. I'm starting to get everyone's names all mixed up in my head. Plus, it's kind of hard to join the conversation when no one can hear you."

Arianne was immediately sorry she'd snapped at Andy. She looked up at his handsome face—the face of the guy she loved more than anyone in the world. Or out of it. He'd moved heaven and—Well, never mind what he'd moved to be with her. He'd done it. Because she needed him. Because she loved him. But just as she reached up to touch his cheek, she saw

Wendy sprinting across the quad toward them. She dropped her hand.

"Oh, hey," Wendy said. "I saw you all the way over here by yourself, and just wanted to make sure you were doing okay."

"She's sweet," Andy said. "You got a good roommate, L.M."

Ari flashed Wendy an appreciative smile. "Yeah, I'm okay. I was just—taking a breather. You having fun?"

"Uh-huh. Just hope no one quizzes us on everyone's names afterward. That'll be the first test I fail in college."

"You and me both," replied Ari.

"Hey, I saw you talking to that musician guy over there," Wendy said. "He's pretty cute."

"Yeah. I mean, I guess," Ari said without looking at Andy. Actually, she did think he was cute.

"And one of the guys from the quad is sort of a babe," Wendy went on. "A little spacey, though. Have you met those guys yet?"

"One of them. Or two of them, I think. Round-faced Korean guy. And that football player with the shaved head. *Neither* of them is babe material," Ari added a little uncomfortably as she caught Andy's mischievous grin.

A little while later, when Wendy had gone off to join an impromptu game of Frisbee and Ari and Andy were alone again, she wasn't at all surprised to catch some teasing. "Babe material, huh? Is that how you talk about us when we're not around to hear?"

"Hey, that was girl talk. Seems like cheating somehow that you got to hear it."

"You mean, like, maybe we need to make a few rules? Starting with Number One: no listening in when you're rating guys?"

"Andy, you're a ten in my book, I promise," Ari said with a wink. "But, yeah, I guess some things are girls only."

"Okay, okay. When I hear it coming, I'll make myself scarce. At least, as far as you can tell!" Andy chuckled.

Ari gave him a light sock in the arm, and she could feel their energy connect.

"All right. I'll vamoose when I'm supposed to. Scout's honor. On all those dumb badges I have hanging on my Cub Scouts uniform."

"Okay," Ari said. "But don't go anywhere now." She put her hand in his and felt a sense of wholeness that had been missing all summer. "Oh, Andy, I've missed you so much. It's so good to be with you again."

"Same here, L.M."

"Listen," Ari suggested, "how about we call the barbecue quits and go check out the rest of the campus?"

Andy nodded. "Your wish is my command."

six

They were whispering so they wouldn't wake Wendy up.
At least, Ari was whispering. Andy could talk as
loudly as he wanted, since Wendy couldn't hear him.
The problem was that Ari would match his volume
without realizing it, and Wendy would stir in her bed
on the other side of the room.

"Shh!" Ari giggled, putting her finger to Andy's
lips. Andy gave it a light, electric-tinged kiss.

It was late and Ari was sleepy, but there was so
much to talk about. Everyone they'd met today. Who
was going to be friends with whom. What classes Ari
wanted to sign up for the next day.

But mostly she just wanted to be with Andy. It
didn't really matter what they were talking about. It
had been the most awesome, incredible day. Ari was
sure lots of people felt that way after their first day at
college. But in her case, it was more amazing than
she could have imagined in her wildest dreams. She
remembered how lonely she'd felt in the car, with her
parents, and this morning seemed light-years away. A
world away. Which it was. She didn't want this day
to end.

She snuggled close to Andy on her bed and felt him wrap her in his magnetic presence. He ran his hand through her hair and down her arm, a tickle of current. She brought her hand to his cheek, feeling how the energy defined the well-chiseled lines of the features she loved. He moved his hands over her body. She tingled at his touch. She brought her lips up to his, and they met in a deep, unhurried kiss.

It was familiar yet different. The comfortable, comforting feeling of kissing the boy she loved, yet with an exciting electricity, a feather-soft charge of newness. The feeling was unlike anything she'd ever experienced. She shivered, losing herself in the sensations. Their kisses grew more intense and passionate. Ari felt as if they must be lighting up the room. She drew him even closer and she heard herself let out a moan of pleasure.

Wendy groaned in response. Ari drew back from their embrace and saw her roommate burrowing her head under her pillow. Ari sighed and rolled away from Andy. "Oops," she whispered.

They lay in silence for a while. Their passions cooled, and Ari felt herself drifting into that relaxed place between wakefulness and sleep. She couldn't fight it any longer. She felt Andy lean over and give her a chaste kiss on the cheek. "Sleep well," he said.

She was warm with happiness. She felt herself giving in to sleep.

Andy could barely remember what it was like to sleep. Or to be sleepy. Or hungry. Or hot or cold. He watched Ari's eyelids get heavy and her eyes close. He heard her breathing slow down, saw her body grow heavy and relaxed. He stretched out next to her and tried to imitate her. But it was no use. It was like spreading an old coat on the bed and expecting the coat to be able to feel what it was like to fall asleep. Sleep was rest for the living body. Once upon a time, it had been as easy as closing his eyes. Now, Andy neither needed sleep nor knew how to achieve it.

He let himself float up so that he was looking at Ari from above. She looked so peaceful, with a gentle smile on her lips—a smile that had been gone for too long. And as he held her sleeping face in his gaze, he knew he was doing the right thing.

He watched her sleep for a while. Then he moved around the room, focusing on different objects, looking at them from the outside and from the inside, figuring out how they were put together. He centered his attention on the clock, wondering if he could do that trick with it again, the one he'd done earlier, while Ari was out getting her registration materials. He felt the electric pulse of his consciousness connect with the flow of electricity through the wires of the clock. He concentrated on slowing down the flow. On stopping it. The liquid crystal display stuck at 2:43. He made the flow move backward. The numbers moved backward, too—2:42, 2:41, 2:40 . . . He let go of his focus for a few moments, and the numbers moved forward again. He gave an extra-hard push with his mind, and the numbers raced ahead. On the clock, an hour passed in a moment.

When he grew tired of playing with the clock, Andy applied himself to Ari's computer. Sure enough, he could tap into its workings, too. Turn it on, turn it off. Log on to the school's server. He'd always been pretty good at tinkering with electronic equipment, anyway. Fixed the family microwave, rigged the coffeemaker to go on just before they all woke up. Stuff like that.

He found his way to his favorite gaming site on the Net and wasted a bunch of time there. Blew away a masterfully large number of evil aliens, amassed a huge cache of secret knowledge.

But when he logged off, it was still dark outside. Dead of night. Which was good in one way. He was finding it hard to spend too much time in the bright sun. As the light went through him, especially the silvery-gold light of a beautiful day, he felt what he had turned his back on, felt the peace and joy, the place where he belonged. And that made it hard to stay rooted to the world in which Ari lived. As they'd explored the campus and town today, there'd been a number of times when it would have been too easy to float right into that field of bliss and never come back.

So, it was still dark outside and Ari was still asleep. And if he wasn't here to be with her, what was the point? He tapped into the current in the stereo system and turned on some music. Very softly. Some mellow jazz.

He imagined the notes as waves of light. And they were! In the space of a thought, the highs and lows, the soft phrases and louder ones, became patterns of light and shadow, moving through the room. Whoa! Cool trick. Better than the clock and computer. Much. He found that with some practice he could shape the lights and shadows at will. Tap his own pure energy into the energy of the light waves. Or something like that.

Basically, he just had to focus, to fix himself on darkening a corner of the room here, illuminating a spot there. Ari's face, for instance. He cast a gentle glow on it. Not enough to disturb her, but now he could really see the beauty of her full lips and classic nose, her closed eyes, the wave of her dark hair.

Whoops! Suddenly one song gave way to another and a blast of Big Band split the silence in the room. Quickly, Andy shut off the music. But Ari groaned loudly and turned over. Andy heard a rustling from Wendy's side of the room. She sat right up in her bed.

"Huh? Ari? What the—" She rubbed her eyes. She checked out Ari, sound asleep again, looked around the room, and fell back down on her pillow.

Andy sighed and let the natural light patterns of the room take over again. There still wasn't a ray of pink in the sky. Maybe he'd wander down the hall and see if anyone else in the dorm was still awake.

$\mathcal{A}$ri *heard Wendy before she was awake enough to focus* on her. "Oh, my god! You really were up all night. I wasn't just dreaming."

Ari blinked a few times and sat up in bed. Wendy's long, red hair was in a wild cloud around her pale, delicate face. Her brow was creased as she stared at Ari.

"No, I wasn't up all night," Ari replied. "Actually, I slept really, really well." It had been the first time, in fact, since . . .

Oh no! Ari thought. *Where is Andy?* Had she dreamed him? Had yesterday been just a strange and wonderful fantasy? She felt her grief begin to overtake her again. But there Andy was, just shimmering into Ari's desk chair over in the darkest corner of the room. Ari felt her spirits give a little jump of joy. She turned her face away from Wendy and blew Andy a secret kiss. He blew one back. "Good morning, beautiful," he said.

It *was* a good morning. Ari swung her legs over the side of the bed and stretched her arms. She felt great. But Wendy was still giving her a funny look.

"If you slept so well, then why is the radio on? And your computer—you didn't shut it off right."

Ari was suddenly aware of the low-level static coming out of the stereo speakers, the radio on but between channels. And sure enough, her computer screen was glowing green in the dim part of the room. Yesterday, Ari hadn't noticed how much darker her side was than Wendy's, even when the sun shone brightly through the large gap where her brown-and-orange curtains weren't fully drawn. The darkness made the computer screen and the power buttons on the stereo seem to glow.

"But everything was off when we went to sleep," Ari said.

"Whoops," Andy confessed. "I guess that's my fault. Entertained myself a little while you were down with the Sandman."

But of course, Wendy hadn't heard what Andy just said. Ari saw an expression of fright cross her roommate's face. "So, if you didn't turn them on, who did?" she asked Ari, her voice wavering.

"Oh. Yeah, well, um, I did wake up just for a little while," Ari improvised hurriedly. Better to cover up for Andy than have Wendy think someone was sneaking into their room. "First-day jitters or something. I listened to a little music, surfed the Web for a bit, and went back to sleep. *Then* I slept well. I hope I didn't bother you," she added, giving Andy a look.

"Really sorry, L.M.," he said.

"Well, I did hear some stuff," Wendy said. "What was that weird computer game you were playing?"

"Lost Treasure of the Rombutars," Andy said.

"Lost Treasure of the Rombutars," Ari echoed.

"Really? You're into that kind of thing?" Wendy sounded very surprised.

"Well, no," Ari said. "I mean, not exactly. I just kind of stumbled across it on-line. Seemed pretty dumb to me, actually." She addressed this last comment in Andy's direction.

Andy just laughed. "Dumb? Lost Treasure? Whoa, baby. I put down a whole alien rebellion while you gals got your beauty sleep. And you do look incredibly lovely today. Did I mention that yet?"

Ari rolled her eyes at him. Trying to sweet-talk his way out of trouble. Just wait till she got him alone. To Wendy, Ari apologized profusely. "I won't disturb you again. I'm really, really sorry."

Wendy shook her head. "No biggie. At home, our next-door neighbor blasts some wicked serious stuff at some ridiculous hours. My folks've called the cops on him a bunch of times. By comparison, that jazz you were playing was basically a lullaby. You have good taste. Even if you don't sleep."

"Why thank you," Andy said.

Ari bit her lip to keep from laughing out loud. Dorm living was going to be interesting, indeed.

"Well, what am I supposed to do while you're asleep?" Andy asked defensively.

Arianne took a bite of her corn muffin and washed it down with a sip of orange juice. "Look, Andy, I'm totally, one hundred percent happy you're here. But I don't think Wendy signed up for a haunted dorm room, you know?"

They had taken their breakfast outside to a patch of grass behind the dining hall so that they could talk freely. Or rather, Ari had taken her breakfast. Andy was just along for the ride. They had a view of Central Bowl, the main green around which the CNE campus was laid out, from where they sat. It was flanked on one side by the stately CNE Learning Center—otherwise known as the library—a cavernous building of heavy stone, and on an adjoining side by the low, modern building that housed the mail room, the student union, and many of the administrative offices. Several other classroom buildings, connected by a network of narrow walkways that cut across the grass, surrounded the bowl.

It was another hot, sunny day. But Andy seemed to be able to make some sort of shade around himself, and Ari sat close to him, taking advantage of its cooling effects.

"I was really trying to be careful not to wake you guys up," Andy said. "You gotta blame it on the DJ at that radio station. I mean, who ever heard of Big Band at four o'clock in the morning?"

"And that Lost Treasure business?"

"Oh. Well, I guess I got a little carried away. I think I set some kind of record," Andy said.

Arianne just looked at him steadily.

"Okay, okay. I'm not going to play around in the room at night anymore. Promise. Anyway, I think the guys in the quad are into the old up-at-night, sleep-all-day routine. At least they were up at a pretty unreasonable hour last night. I guess I could go hang with them if I wanted."

Ari felt a pinch of guilt. "I mean, I don't want to seem like I'm kicking you out or anything. It's just—"

Andy waved a shimmery hand. "Totally understandable, L.M. It's cool. Really."

Ari smiled at him. "You're the best."

"Out of this world, huh?" Andy kidded.

45

Ari swallowed the last bite of muffin. "Silly," she said with an affectionate giggle. "Trust you to make a joke out of being dead." The giggle died on her lips. She hadn't meant to say that. It had slipped out. And it wasn't funny. Not at all. She looked into Andy's glimmery-sheer face and she felt a warm sting of tears fill her eyes.

He passed his weightless fingers over her eyelids, as if to wipe away the tears. The electric tingle was comforting, but it couldn't do the job of flesh and blood. The tears pooled and made their way down her cheeks.

"Ari. Arianne," he whispered. "It's okay, Ari, it's really not so bad. Shh, baby. All right, let it out." He enveloped her in his magnetic grasp, and she felt herself sobbing. Andy simply held her, and she felt a kind of pulsing, rocking motion. It helped to soothe her, and finally her sobs ebbed.

"It isn't so awful, is it?" Andy asked. "We're together. That's the important thing."

Arianne looked around her. The campus was starting to fill up with students as the first day of classes drew nearer. People crisscrossed the walkways from one building to another. You could spot the new kids by a certain intent look, as they studied their surroundings and formed mental maps of the campus. The old hands, at school early to help with freshman orientation, seemed to have a clearer goal in mind, though they frequently stopped to greet friends after the long summer. A striking girl with dark skin and a short, white sundress threw her arms around a beanpole-thin guy with spiky black hair and black clothes. The girl then did an about-face and walked off with the guy in the same direction from which she'd come. Sitting off on the sidelines with Andy, Arianne felt distanced from the rest of her new schoolmates.

"I can go if you want me to," Andy said tentatively.

Arianne was seized with panic. "Go?" Every nerve in her body resisted the thought. The emptiness and loneliness of her summer were fresh wounds. She could still feel the ache of imitating the moves of getting through a day. She'd longed for the release of the night, but the darkness had only left her more alone with her pain. What was being a little outside of the crowd, compared to that?

She took Andy's hand and felt the race of electricity. She thought about the first time she'd seen him. The first day of eleventh grade, third period bio. He was the new kid, moved from a different part of the state when his father got transferred. He wandered into the classroom a few minutes late, looking lost. Lost but totally adorable in a sky-blue T-shirt the color of his eyes, his hair streaked with gold from a summer in the sun.

"Whoa, the new guy's cute," Loren had said. As if Ari could miss it. She and Andy had caught each other's eye the instant he'd walked into the room. She could feel the attraction right away.

Now, as she looked into his eyes, the powerful connection was still there. Still strong enough to bridge the gap between two worlds. She remembered that silly strawberry jam heart on toast he'd made for her on their last night. How all summer long she'd wished she'd wrapped it up and taken it home.

But it hadn't been their last night, after all. Because here they were, together. Ari was swept up by the strength of her luck and of her love. "No, don't go," she begged him. "Stay with me. Please."

"Sure?" Andy asked gently.

"Sure," Ari answered.

eight

Ari checked over her course selection and made sure she'd filled out all the right forms and cards. Andy had been urging her toward more math and science, the kinds of practical classes he would have chosen, but Ari wanted to do more experimenting now, which would help her figure out where she was going later.

Theater Improv was number one on her list. She was also signing up for Intro to Art History, Psychology 101, Literature of Myth, and Human Biology—the one course she and Andy had agreed on. She was scheduled for swim team tryouts, and if she could squeeze it in, she wanted to be part of the CNE chorus, too. She only hoped her first choices weren't full by the time she got to the front of the interminable line that snaked around the basement room. She shuffled forward a few baby steps.

If Andy had been here, he could have kept her amused by peeking over people's shoulders and reading off their class selections. She could imagine them betting on who was signing up for Rocks for Jocks. Ari picked out the big moose of a guy up near the front who could easily be going for a few easy geology credits. Of course, you never knew. His schedule could be full of courses like Modern Philosophy and Advanced Russian. The girl with the neo-Woodstock clothes and the dangly silver jewelry? Definitely the English major type.

But Ari didn't have a secret pair of eyes this morning to confirm or deny her suspicions about her new classmates. Andy figured his days of waiting in lines were over, and he'd promised to meet her back at the dorm later.

It was probably just as well. Ari had lots of chores to do. Checking out the jobs at student employment, getting her CNE photo ID, finding her box in the mail room . . . Besides, if Andy had been around making jokes in her ear, she would have stood in line laughing like a loony tune. The registration people probably would have found her mentally unfit to attend classes.

"So, what're you taking this semester?"

Ari swiveled around to see the guitar player from the Eakens picnic. "Oh, hi!" she said, looking up at him. Warm brown eyes, dark curls, a distinct, angular face, a catchy smile. Wendy was right about the guy. He was cute. Ari felt herself blush. Good thing Andy wasn't around to see. She held out her class selection form so he could look at it.

"Oh, hey, cool. I'm signing up for Literature of Myth, too," he said. "Professor Greenburg's supposed to be really smart. Really tough, too, but good. My sister had him when she was here."

"Yeah? That's good to know. I just like the course description." Ari flipped to the dog-eared page in the course catalog she was holding with her papers and forms. " 'Reality concealed in poetic image and story,' " she quoted. "Kind of a cool definition, don't you think?"

"Maybe more like reality *revealed* through poetic image and story," the boy said. "Or maybe it's not reality at all. Maybe it's just some nice, packaged-up story that isn't true at all, because reality is just too totally weird for anyone to believe."

Ari thought about Andy for a moment. "It sure is," she agreed. "You sound like maybe you're a philosophy major."

"Majorly undecided," the boy said. "There's just too much I haven't tried yet to narrow it down to one thing."

Ari smiled. She could relate. "So . . . if you don't mind my asking a question from the Orientation Rag, what is your name anyway?"

The boy grinned. "Yeah, we didn't ever get to that, did we? I'm Ben. And I come from Boston, and I did okay on my SATs, even though I think they're not good for measuring much of anything."

Ari laughed. "Hi, Ben. I'm Ari. I'm from Portwater. I think they should outlaw the SATs, too."

"Portwater! I spent a vacation there a few summers ago. It's really beautiful."

"Yeah, it is."

"I was sort of jealous of the people who got to live there all year long."

"It gets kind of quiet in the winter," Ari said. "I mean, really quiet. I like it, but most people go a little nuts. I like Boston, too. Especially all the theaters and movies. And the people performing on the street—that's my favorite part."

Ben smiled broadly. "Yeah, me, too. You ever see that mime with the red stripe on his face? He hangs out near the Commons."

"You mean the one who juggles, too? Oh, wow, he's really good," Ari said.

"Yeah, he's got a good act," Ben agreed. "That's cool that you've seen him. You go into Boston a lot?"

"Pretty often. My cousin lives in Brookline. He's a dentist. Dr. Zweig."

"Oh, my god! Dr. Zweig!" Ben waited a beat. "No, I don't know him," he said, his delivery perfectly timed.

Okay, so here she was in line, laughing like a loony tune, anyway. Almost before she was ready, they were up at the front. "Well, see you back at the dorm," she told Ben.

"Definitely. I'm in room 304," he answered. "My roommate's name is Todd."

"Cool," Ari said. She stopped short of telling him what room she was in, given that she had both an official and an unofficial roommate. It could be kind of weird if Ben stopped by while Andy was there.

"Why is it that photo IDs, driver's licenses, and passport photos all look like mug shots?" Ari asked as she held out her new university ID for Andy to see. "Prisoner number 08674, arrested for closing her eyes in front of the camera and not brushing her hair."

Andy laughed. "You look beautiful as always, L.M. You just look like you dozed off for a few minutes there. Don't tell me your first full day at CNE was that boring."

"Actually, it was kind of fun for a bunch of chores." Ari pushed aside a pile of Wendy's clothes and sat down cross-legged on the floor of her dorm room. "I'm starting to get an idea of where everything is around here. And I kept bumping into people from the dorm. You won't believe who Wendy and I shared a table with at lunch. That girl Leslie. You know, Luggage Lady? And her roommate, Marla. She's from Connecticut. They both turned out to be pretty nice. I'm just not sure how Leslie managed to get all over campus in those spike-heeled sandals. Stayed off the grass, I guess," Ari said with a laugh. "She just needs to lose her glam act."

"The guys in the quad like it," Andy said. He was stretched out on the bed. "They'd like to see her lose those fancy threads, for sure, but definitely not in the same way you mean it."

"Andy!" Ari said severely.

"Hey, their opinion, not mine," he said.

"How do you know?"

"They were talking about it last night. I sort of popped in on them to see who was awake."

"Well, they sound totally crude," Ari admonished.

Andy laughed. "You have your girl talk and they have their boy talk."

Ari opened her mouth to say that it was different, but maybe it wasn't. At least not that much. Besides, she didn't want to bother fighting about those jerks in the quad. Not when she was in such a good mood. "Well, anyway, Leslie's okay," she said. "That's all I really meant."

"That guy Ben seems nice, too," Andy said.

Ari tensed up. "Wait a minute. How'd you know I was talking to Ben?" Her face flushed hot with anger. She felt as if Andy had been peering in the window on the sly. "Were you following me around all day?"

Andy looked hurt. "No, I just checked in on you a few times."

But Ari was still annoyed. "Andy, I thought I left my parents back home," she said.

Andy climbed off the bed and came to sit next to her. "I just wanted to make sure you were okay. You've been so sad since—well, you know, and I'm here to change that. I only wanted to see for myself if you were happy."

Arianne felt the sincerity of Andy's words, his caring and love. She felt her anger melting away. "Andy, I am happy. Since you've been here, I mean." She turned her face toward his and gave him a kiss. She felt the electric thrill. "I love you, Andy," she whispered. "I really do."

"I love you too, L.M. And from here on in, no more Mom."

"I like that idea. One mom's enough, right?" Ari patted Andy's leg. "So, where did you go today? When you weren't with me." A silent voice in her head wondered if he'd gone wherever people went after they—

No! She didn't even want to entertain the thought. If she let it into her head, she'd start thinking about how impossible this whole thing was and she was sure she would lose Andy for good.

But Andy just slung a charged arm around her. "I don't know. I checked out the library and media lab and the AV room. Watched a bunch of videos. Popped in on a planning meeting at the science department. I can tell you which teachers seem like the good ones and which ones definitely to avoid."

Andy paused for a moment. "Wait. Maybe not. I said I'd give up the mom thing, right? So you go ahead and figure it all out on your own. I don't want you to miss out on any of your college experience, Ari. I honestly don't."

"So does that mean you think my Human Bio professor stinks?" Ari asked, laughing.

"Nah, she seemed fine," Andy said, laughing along. "Oh, and hey, speaking of your college experience, here comes Wendy. Why don't you guys hang for a while without me? It's kinda weird being an invisible third wheel."

"Well, if it's all right with you," Ari said. Andy nodded. "I guess I'll go to dinner with her. I mean, since you're not big on meals anymore anyway."

Sure enough, she heard the doorknob rattle, and Wendy walked in. "Hey, roomie," Ari greeted her. She glanced around and Andy was gone.

nine

Ari and Wendy carried their dinner trays over to the same table where they'd eaten lunch. It looked like it was going to be their spot—a table near the window, looking out onto grassy Central Bowl. Leslie and Marla had arrived first and were already holding court with Larry and Bill.

Ari sat next to Larry. He'd left the Cat in the Hat headgear home tonight, but it was impossible for her not to notice that everything on his plate was red: chicken cutlet smothered in tomato sauce; beets; a dish of cherry Jell-O; and a glass of some kind of berry-colored juice.

"What happened to eating low on the food chain?" she asked.

Larry shrugged. "I don't know. Not decorative enough for me. This—well, it makes an aesthetic statement, you know?"

"Jell-O is not an aesthetic statement," Leslie said with a note of disdain. She took a bite of her salad— the only thing on her plate besides a hard-boiled egg and half an apple.

"And beets? Ugh," Marla added.

"I don't love 'em myself," Larry admitted, "but, hey, sometimes you've gotta sacrifice for fashion. Leslie, you of all people know what I mean."

Leslie rolled her eyes. But Larry had a point. She had taken the concept of dressing for dinner to the hilt. In a sea of jeans and T-shirts, she was the only one draped in a slinky midnight-blue slip dress. Very Caroline Bessette-Kennedy.

"In fact, I was thinking of doing white foods tomorrow night," Larry went on. "Leslie, maybe you want to put on that white number from the picnic again, and we could match."

"Lar, you're a moron," Bill said mildly. He had a very normal burger and fries on his tray.

"Leslie, I think you look great," Wendy put in. "It's nice to have some elegance at our table. No offense to the strikingly red palette of your dinner, Larry."

"People just don't understand the creative mind," Larry deadpanned.

Ari couldn't decide if he was funny or just obnoxious. Both, she guessed. She took a bite of chicken cutlet, her choice, too. The food was so nondescript that you might as well choose by color.

"Oh, hey, there's Corinne," Bill said, waving over the French girl they'd met at the picnic. Corinne was just coming from the cafeteria food line, carefully balancing her dinner tray.

They made room for Corinne at the table, and she and Bill immediately started talking in fluent French. Ari was surprised. Bill seemed like the most normal, typical, all-American guy. But it turned out his family had lived for a number of years in Grenoble, in the French Alps.

It was fun getting to know so many new people at once. They were quickly joined by Shelly from across the hall, and then all squeezed in as tightly as they could, taking the food off their trays and stacking the trays on the floor, to make room for Cesar and Mike from upstairs. Several conversations were going at once, and the chatter was loud and happy.

Ari and Wendy discovered that Leslie was into acting, too, and they launched into a discussion about who'd played which role in what high school play. "Oh, my god, you were Maria in *West Side Story*, too?" Leslie asked her. They immediately broke into a chorus of "Tonight" to the applause of everyone at the table.

Later, Ari and Bill tried to calculate their chances of making the swim team, while Larry, Mike, and Wendy swapped Lollapollooza stories.

Finally, Ari just sat back for a while and listened to everyone else talk. "Oh, wow, you heard the Presidio Beach show, too?" Wendy was asking Mike. "You mean, you actually came all the way from Colorado for that show!? Cool! I wonder if we were sitting anywhere near each other."

Ari was mildly amazed that a few days ago none of them had known a thing about one another. Now, they were already starting to feel like a group of friends. At the two dozen or so large, round tables in the room, people were talking animatedly in pairs or groups. A few kids had their noses in books as they ate. A gray cloud marked the smoking section at the far end of the dining hall. Ari didn't feel separate from the crowd tonight.

She felt herself grow alert as she spotted a tall, thin guy with curly, dark hair over by the salad bar, his back to her. Ben? He turned. No. Definitely not. She felt a beat of disappointment. But it got lost as she listened to Cesar and Shelly debating the merits of roller blading versus mountain biking.

After dinner, as she and Wendy were bussing their trays at the far end of the cafeteria, Mike came over and said they were all going to head over to the student union. "Hang out, play some pool, whatever. You guys want to come?"

"Sure," Wendy said. She set her tray down on the conveyer belt and it slid away through the low opening in the wall that led to the kitchen. "Don't we, Ari?"

Suddenly, Arianne felt tugged in two directions. Her high spirits dipped. "You go ahead, Wendy." Ari got rid of her dinner tray. "I—have some stuff to do back at the dorm."

"Aw, come on, Ari," Wendy said.

"Yeah, it won't be a party without you," Mike added.

Arianne wanted to go. But what if Andy was waiting for her back at the room? Then she heard the words he'd spoken earlier echoing in her head. *I don't want you missing out on any of your college experience, Ari. Honestly, I don't.*

"Well . . . okay, I'll come," Ari said. She only hoped that Andy wouldn't mind.

The student union was definitely downscale. Worn, greenish indoor/outdoor carpeting under a low ceiling; a wall of vending machines selling drinks and snack food; another wall sporting a huge bulletin board covered with a chaotic patchwork of flyers and signs; a couple of video games. The tables and chairs didn't match. Not even close. Still, the atmosphere was relaxed and easy. There was a good jukebox. An old Stones tune was pumping as they walked in. But the epicenter of the student union was the pool table. Freshmen and upperclassmen met over stiff eight ball competition at the green-felt-covered table. Looked like a few high school kids from town had sneaked in, too.

Ari felt comfortable as they sat down. The student union reminded her a bit of a bar called the Keg House back in Portwater. The long, wooden bar at the Keg House was scarred and sticky from beer, but the place sported the same mismatched furniture and the same focus on the pool table as the student union. They weren't really supposed to go to the Keg House until they turned twenty-one. And in the summer, when it was packed and IDs were checked extra-carefully, they didn't bother. But in the winter, when it was just people from town, the management usually let them in for a couple of games of pool as long as they didn't drink or get too rowdy. Andy had taught her the finer points of the game, and she wasn't bad.

"I think I'll put my name up for a game," she announced.

"You go, girl!" Wendy said, sounding impressed.

"Woman power," Larry concurred goofily.

"Cool. Put my name up, too?" Mike asked. "I'll get everyone a bunch of sodas and some chips."

"Okay." Ari got up and headed for the blackboard on the wall by the pool table. She picked up the chalk and printed their names under the two already on the list. *Ari. Mike.* She felt a tug of anguish. *Ari. Andy.* That's how she was used to signing up for a pool game. *Andy. Ari.* Loser has to take the winner to dinner. Winner has to give the loser a consolation kiss.

Arianne sighed as she put the chalk back. Andy wasn't going to be hitting any cue balls again. Playing computer games with his electric aura, or whatever it was he'd tried to explain to her, was one thing. Radios, clocks, lights, electrical appliances . . . Moving solid pool balls was another. No way he was going to send those babies rolling just by thinking about it. On the other hand, he'd probably like the student union. Next time, maybe he'd want to come along.

Ari watched the game that was going on now. A guy in a brand-new CNE sweatshirt against a scrawny kid who barely looked old enough to be in high school. Definitely not a CNE student. But he was good. Excellent. He wasn't missing a shot. Ari watched him line the angles up with his eyes and then sink one ball after another. He called the eight ball in one of the corner pockets, took a clean shot, and the game was over. He looked at his friends, at a nearby table, and put his cue stick down on the pool table just long enough to clasp his hands together over his head in victory.

"Well, you better win," one of his friends called back. "You sleep with that cue stick, Ty." Everyone at the table laughed.

The kid beat his next two opponents in record time. He looked at the blackboard. "Ari?" he called.

Ari stepped up to the table and introduced herself. "Hey, Ari. Tyler," he said.

Ari put all the balls back on the table and racked them up. Then she chose a cue stick and rubbed the tip with a cube of blue chalk. She nodded at Tyler. He crouched level with the table and made a few little back-and-forth motions with his stick. He broke with a shot that sank several balls at once. He called stripes, and proceeded to sink several more. Ari was beginning to think he might win without her taking a single shot.

But finally he missed one, and the table was hers. She heard a whistle from her friends' direction, and she saw she had a cheering squad. Wendy flashed her a thumbs-up. Leslie crossed the shabby room in her slinky blue dress and stood near the table to watch. The girl was a trip. Like a Hollywood star in the middle of the run-down room.

Ari lined up her shot. "Middle pocket, right," she said. Boom. She sank it.

Cheers from the peanut gallery. "Nice," Tyler said.

She missed the next one, but so did Tyler. She sank another. He wound up winning again, but Ari lost very respectably. "Appreciate some good comp once in a while," Tyler complimented her. She handed her cue stick over to Mike and headed back over to join the rest of the gang.

"Good going," Wendy said.

"Thanks." Ari grinned and helped herself to a soda. "But I couldn't beat the house champ."

Tyler took Mike down pretty fast, too. Even with Wendy over by the pool table cheering him on. She and Mike came back to join the rest of them, pulling up chairs beside Ari. "You really know how to play," Mike said to her. "Who taught you to sink those balls?"

"Oh, um, my boyfriend," Ari said a little uncomfortably. "We shot a bunch of pool at this place back home." She saw Wendy flash her a sympathetic look.

"Ah-hah! So you left your heart in Portwater?" Larry said. He hummed a few notes of "I Left My Heart in San Francisco." Wendy gave him a silencing stare, but he didn't seem to notice.

Ari felt herself tensing up. "Well, no. Not really," she said.

"Oh, he's off at a different school?" Larry persisted.

"Um, no." Well, he wasn't.

"You're not together," Larry concluded. "Or you decided to see other people when you went away."

There was quiet at the table. A drum riff from the jukebox measured the pause. Ari and Wendy traded glances. Finally, Ari said, "He died." Her words hung in the air. The mood was instantly somber.

"Oh, god, Ari, I'm really sorry," Larry said sincerely. "I *am* a moron. Bill is right."

Ari swallowed hard. "You didn't know."

"That's really awful," Shelly said.

"You poor thing," Leslie murmured.

"It's okay. Really," Ari told them. "I—how can I explain this? I'm never going to lose what he and I have. Had. Whatever."

"It's good you're going on with your life," Marla said softly.

"Yes," Corinne agreed. "We're glad you are here with us."

It took a while for the party to get going again.

Ari was wiped out, but happily so. She lay in bed, going over the long day and even longer night. After a few more games of pool at the student union, the whole gang had paraded over to the Bean and Bass Coffee House, on South Quad, trying to hit all the campus spots in one night.

She thought about Leslie, in her fashion plate dress, her feet bare on the campus greens, her strappy sandals swinging in one hand. Ari and Wendy had decided that Leslie was like Ginger on *Gilligan's Island*—the starlet marooned with a bunch of regular folk.

Well, Larry wasn't exactly regular folk, either. He'd gone for the red fruit punch at the student union, and the red zinger tea at the coffeehouse, and asked the girl strumming her acoustic guitar on the coffeehouse's tiny stage if she knew how to play "Red Cadillac."

Ari had ordered a peppermint tea, and Wendy had read her tea leaves. The cozy, dark room with cushiony chairs and couches and small, low tables was the right place for it.

"I see new horizons opening. Yeah, I know—duh. And the way the leaves are kind of clustered over here? Means you're going to be getting into something really new. A new project or hobby or something."

"And how about the tall, dark, mysterious stranger?" Bill had kidded, leaning over his double latte and chocolate chip cookie.

"Well, I don't know about tall, dark, or mysterious," Wendy replied. "But there's definitely a big romance going on in these leaves." She'd looked at Ari and grinned.

In fact, Ari had a feeling the romance was in Wendy's cup. She couldn't help noticing how close Wendy and Mike moved to each other as Wendy read his leaves.

Now, back in her room in bed, Ari snuggled farther under the covers. Romance. She wondered sleepily where Andy was anyway. And then, suddenly, she didn't feel sleepy at all. Had Andy left? *I can go if you want me to.* Ari had gone out with her new friends and had fun. Without him. Had he taken it as a sign?

Her body tensed, her pulse started pumping. And then, as if he could feel her discomfort, there he was, leaning over her, kissing her brow.

"Mmm, Andy," she murmured, tired and happy again. "I was just falling asleep."

"Did you have a good time?" he whispered.

Ari nodded. "Tell you all about it in the morning. You don't mind, do you? Lots to do tomorrow. I gotta get a good night's sleep."

"No problem," Andy whispered back. "Good night, L.M."

She fell asleep in his embrace.

"*W*asted *again!*" Andy admonished the guys in the quad. "Don't you party animals know when to quit?"

But Rodney, Dave, Eugene, and Sean were unaware of his presence and deaf to his words. The living room that connected the two double bedrooms was strewn with empty cans, Twinkies wrappers, and dirty socks. One of the pea-green curtains had come partway down, and it hung like a flag at half-mast over the window. In only a couple of days, the guys had trashed the place.

Andy floated over to where Dave sat drinking a beer on the sofa, his meaty legs splayed. He rubbed Dave's shiny, shaved dome. "Few more of those, my friend, and the football coach is going to tell you to take a hike."

As if he'd felt a tickle, Dave reached up and scratched his head. Then he let out a loud belch.

"Nice, fella," Andy commented.

Next to Dave sat Eugene, poring over the Incoming Students Booklet. It was essentially a collection of the new students' ID photos. Their names were printed under their pictures, arranged in alphabetical order. The booklet was supposed to help the freshmen and transfers get to know who was who. But Eugene was going through the booklet with a red pen, drawing a circle around all the girls he thought were pretty.

"Big ones," he'd written next to one of them. Andy peered over Eugene's left shoulder; Dave peered over the other. "How do you know that, pal?" Dave asked. "It only shows her from the head up."

"I saw her, okay? She lives in that dorm over next to the library," Eugene said. "And believe me . . ." He made a lewd gesture with his hands.

From what Andy had already seen of Eugene, he was intent on breaking every rule or moral code his strict Korean immigrant parents probably had ever imposed on him. "Doing good, buddy," Andy commented. "You're well on your way to being a genuine, first-class American pig."

Over in the armchair, Sean was slumped as if he was asleep, a cigarette burning down to a long ash on the top of his beer can. He was the one Wendy thought was sort of a babe. Andy doubted she'd think so if she saw him now. Sean opened one bloodshot eye and peered at Dave and Eugene. "Neck up only? Well, here's an idea. Do our own Incoming Students Booklet. An underground version. Girls only. Full body shots. Put their phone numbers, too. Sell 'em on the campus black market."

"Campus black market?" This from Dave.

"Sure," Eugene put in. "Every empire's got a black market. Good idea, Sean. Every guy on campus'll buy it."

"Yo, man, don't you dudes talk about anything but the ladies?" Rodney asked. He sat on the floor, his back against the wall, pressing buttons on a pocket video game.

"What else is there, man?" asked Sean. "Wine, women, and song." Though actually the CD on the stereo had finished playing quite some time ago. "What's the matter, Rod, you're not into women?"

" 'Course I am, man. But I don't need to talk about them all the time. I know the ladies like me. I'm secure with my women, know what I'm saying?"

"Right, that's why you're here hanging with us," Dave said sarcastically.

Andy gave a short laugh. "You guys are jerks," he said. But at least they were jerks who were awake. Everyone else in Eakens was off in cloud-cuckoo land. Well, except for one couple on whom Andy didn't exactly think it would be polite to drop in.

"Yo, look at her. Check this one out," Eugene said, stabbing his index finger at a picture.

Andy looked. Rebecca Mitchum. Shoulder-length, pale blond hair; big smile; big blue eyes. Yeah, she was pretty. Suzanne Moore was even prettier, with toffee-colored skin and close-cropped hair that framed her full, perfectly even features.

But wait! *What the heck am I doing?* Andy wondered. These guys were getting to him. He had the most beautiful, wonderful girlfriend in the world a few doors down. The only problem was that she was sound asleep.

He drifted over to Rodney and zeroed in on his video game, a car that you tried to make run over as many people as possible. Andy focused on the car with his mind and seized control. He took it for a ride around the edge of the mini-screen. Rodney punched buttons furiously, then shook the whole game hard. Andy let go, and Rodney went back to systematically killing the crudely rendered pedestrians. No Lost Treasures, for sure.

Then Andy concentrated on the stereo. Okay, maybe he'd do his hosts a favor. Put on some more music, since they were too wasted and lazy to do it themselves. He switched from CD mode to the radio. Found a station playing alternative rock. Switched the radio on and let loose a loud blast of steely guitar and drums.

The guys nearly jumped out of their seats. "Whoa!" Sean came to life and knocked over his beer can. The stale yellow liquid seeped into the rug. "Who did that?" He managed to get out of his chair, then went over to the stereo and looked at it suspiciously.

"What's going on, man? What's happening over there?" Rodney asked, his voice shaky.

Sean raised his shoulders. "Dunno. Somehow the radio went on." He continued to stare at the stereo. Andy's silent laughter filled the room. "It just . . . I don't know, but it did," Sean muttered.

"Well, at least it's a cool tune," Mike said with a nervous guffaw. He made an air guitar with his hand and strummed a chord.

This seemed to relax them all a little. Sean oozed back into his chair. Andy immediately change the station.

"And the Lord sayeth that thou shalt never, never . . ." came a deep, resonant voice from the speakers.

Andy grinned. Good choice. Rodney dropped his game, jumped up, and raced over to the stereo console. "What the—" He fiddled furiously with the channel dial until he got the rock station back. "Dave, what is wrong with this freaking thing?"

Dave was pale. He looked like he'd just gotten pounced on by the entire opposing team. "I dunno. It worked fine back home," he said hoarsely.

"Thing's a piece of junk," Rodney said. He fixed it with a look, as if to keep it on the right station.

"I don't know, maybe it's our energy," Sean suggested, his words slurred. "My brothers and I had this car once. Actually, it was our old man's car, but we basically monopolized it, so he had to get himself another one. Anyway, this one time we were cruising around and we were wa-sted! I'm talking the whole liquor cabinet. The whole medicine cabinet. The whole stash. We were seeing stuff. Hearing stuff. Little trails of light coming off anything that moved. You could feel the energy when we got into the car. Like there was too much of it or something. Before we even turn on the ignition, boom! One of the windows just shatters. All by itself. I swear. To let out some of that energy."

"Kept you fools off the road," Rodney said, pressing a button and doing some damage with his own joke of a car.

"Someone probably threw a rock at you," Dave said.

"No way, man," said Sean. "You think someone just threw a rock at that stereo? It's the energy, I'm telling you. En-er-gy!"

Well, he was right about the energy, Andy thought.

The guys stared at the stereo blankly. The rock music coming out of it was the only sound for a while. Eventually, they went back to whatever they had been doing. Spacing out. Sean popped the top off another warm beer. "Want one?" He tossed a couple to the other guys. "Hey, Dave, you got any more smoke?"

"Naw. We did it all up," Dave said.

Andy felt himself getting bored again. He dimmed the light in the room, then made it brighter, then dimmed it again. Rodney blinked. Eugene rubbed his eyes. But it was too subtle for these stoners. Andy did it again. Faster, with more intensity. A burst of strobe. The four roommates' faces lit up and disappeared and lit up again.

Andy could feel them snap to. "Hey!" Dave yelped. The guys exchanged muddy-headed glances. They looked around the room nervously, as if they might find an answer for what was happening. Andy had their attention. He tried the less-blatant approach again, swirling a little pattern of light and shadow through the air, a smokelike wisp, curling and diving lazily.

"Oh, my god," Eugene said in a low voice.

"Dave, what was in that stuff anyway?" Sean asked.

Rodney's game lay useless in his hands. Dave buried his face in his palms. He picked up his head to take another peak. Andy shortened and lengthened the light waves, turning his drifting patterns red, then blue, then purple.

"It's a freaking light show," Sean breathed. "Are you guys seeing what I'm seeing?"

They could barely nod.

Andy entertained them for a while longer. Finally, the sun started coming up. At last. People would be waking up soon. Well, the ones who'd gone to sleep, that was.

When Dave and Sean and Rodney and Eugene were finally able to talk again, they all agreed they'd better ease up on the partying.

Arianne's alarm clock went off early. She groaned and slapped the off button. She managed to get one eye open, stretch her arms and legs, and get the other eye open, too. She wanted to get in a workout in the CNE pool before breakfast, while the aqua-colored, Olympic-sized lanes were still mostly empty

It had been terribly hard to get back into the water after the accident. Just wading in the ocean made her remember the power of the riptide, and panic overwhelmed her. She'd had to begin in the little pool in Loren's backyard, and even then her heart had pounded in her throat and she couldn't catch her breath. Besides, she'd just been too miserable to really work out. But now that she was feeling so good, she wanted to get herself back in top form. Or close enough for the swim team trials at the end of next week.

She sat up and swung her legs over the side of the bed. Wendy slept soundly, her red hair fanned out against the white of her pillow. A few weak rays of sun filtered around the curtains. A bird chirped outside. The room was quiet. Peaceful. No static from the stereo, no lights mysteriously on. Didn't look as if Andy had spent much time in the room while they'd been sleeping.

Right on cue, he floated through the door. Ari felt herself come more fully awake. She still wasn't quite used to his unorthodox entrances. "Good morning, L.M." He smiled brightly. "I thought that was you getting up." He came over and gave her a kiss on the cheek. It felt like a fresh, morning breeze.

"Mmm, good morning yourself," she said as softly as possible, glancing over at Wendy's sleeping form. "My favorite night owl. Where've you been?"

Andy gave a wave of his hand. "Oh, here and there. Around. Down the hall at the quad for a while."

72

"Oh." Ari felt a beat of displeasure. "With those jerks who should only be so lucky to have Leslie even say hi to them?"

Andy shrugged. "I know, but hey, they were awake. I just listened to a little music with them . . ." He paused. "Stuff like that. Ari, everyone else in this whole dorm was down for the count, you know?"

Arianne heard the plaintive note creep into his voice. She suddenly had a glimmer of how it was from his side. Wow, the nights probably could get pretty lonely. She patted his hand. "Well, I'm up now," she said.

Wendy stirred.

Ari dropped her voice to the barest whisper. "But let's let Wendy sleep." She pulled on some clothes and a pair of sandals; grabbed her knapsack; stuffed her swimsuit, cap, and goggles into it; and she and Andy left the room in the more conventional way.

"Going to check out the pool?" Andy asked when they were out in the hall.

Ari nodded. "Wanna come?" She let her voice rise to normal speaking level now that they were out of the room. "I could use a cheering section. I know I'm totally out of shape."

"Sure, I'll come. And don't worry. You'll be fine," Andy said encouragingly. "When are tryouts?"

"A week from Friday."

"Piece of cake," Andy said.

"Hope so," Ari said as they passed an early riser coming up the stairs. The girl gave Ari a weird look.

Ari looked down at herself. Had she put her shirt on inside out, trying to get out of the room in a hurry? Slipped on two different shoes? Then she realized what it was. The girl thought that Ari was talking to herself. "Just rehearsing," Ari called up to her.

73

"Memorizing my part for an audition." She looked at Andy and winked, trying not to laugh.

As soon as the girl was out of earshot, she and Andy cracked up.

"Pull!" Andy coached. "Atta girl. Smooth. Bring your right hand down closer to your side. Even out the kick. Uh-huh. Good!"

Arianne swam sleekly through the water. Andy's voice rang deep inside her head, instructing, cajoling, encouraging her best stroke.

Ari had been in a few pools with underwater speakers. Usually that just meant some high-energy tunes pumping through the water in a hollow, echoey sort of way. But Andy's voice came from outside and inside at the same time, as if his coaching was a kind of personal inspiration coming from someplace deep down inside Ari. It made her swim that much harder, stronger, concentrating on keeping her stroke as streamlined as possible.

But it had been a long time, and her arms and legs burned. She could feel her muscles reaching their limit. "Okay, that's four laps. Four more to go," Andy said. "Keep it relaxed. You're doing great."

Ari swam. She concentrated on the sensation of drawing herself through the water, making sure her hands entered the water at the angle of least resistance and didn't make even the tiniest splash, her feet fluttering with small, quick motions, her body level, just cutting the surface of the pool. She turned her head only just enough to take in a breath through the corner of her mouth, tucking it into her neck to create a pocket of air. Breathe. Stroke, stroke, stroke. Breathe. She covered one more lap, two, three. Four. She touched the edge of the pool. Whew! She let her feet touch bottom. She stood up and breathed heavily.

"Okay, L.M. Only one more set. Thirty-second rest. You ready?"

Ari was panting too hard to protest.

"Okay, then. Here goes. Ten, nine, eight . . . three, two, one!"

Ari filled her lungs with air. She sank under the water, grabbing the edge of the pool behind her with one hand. She anchored her feet against the side of the pool and pushed off. Go!

She pictured herself moving forward, pulling against the water as if it were a handhold in a rock and she was a climber going up, up, up. She touched the wall at the deep end and did a neat, graceful flip turn. Last set . . . She gave it everything she had.

Suddenly she felt herself enveloped by Andy's tingly touch, her whole body bathed in it, the two of them moving through the water together. She could feel the force of his love, the power of him around her. She felt a surge of extra strength. She shot through the water like a speedboat. She covered her laps with lightning precision. She sprinted the last half a lap, reached the shallow end, and came up laughing.

"That's why I call you Little Mermaid." Andy was laughing, too. "Good work."

"Good work!" a second voice echoed. Ari swiveled. Standing at the edge of the pool, looking down, was a slender man in his late twenties or early thirties in a blue racing suit, goggles pushed up on his forehead, with close-cropped black hair and broad shoulders. "Dan Michaels. Assistant swim coach. I see you like to get your workout in early, too." He hopped into the lane next to her with a small splash.

"Arianne Kessler," Ari introduced herself. They exchanged a wet handshake.

"You were really focused," he complimented her. "You train that hard every day?"

Ari laughed. "I don't know. I had, well, I kind of found this—extra reserve there at the end. A secret reserve."

"Well, I hope we're going to see you and your secret reserve at team tryouts," Coach Michaels said.

"Definitely," Ari answered.

"Definitely," echoed her secret.

eleven
∠

It was like a day at the beach without the beach. Central
Bowl was dotted with kids soaking up the sun on the
last calm afternoon before classes began. Ari was
even starting to recognize some of the faces. The
group of girls under the huge, leafy maple usually sat
a few tables away in the dining hall. The couple
locked at the lip were already famous for being pri-
vate in public. But there were lots of faces she was
seeing for the first time, too. Now that the semester
was about to start, the upperclassmen were returning,
filling up the campus as if it belonged to them. The
bowl was busier than it had been all week. The pace
had changed, as if someone had turned some invisible
dial.

Ari and Wendy sat on the grass in the middle of
the action. Perfect seats for hanging out and watching
the CNE show. Next to them, a dark-haired girl in a
tiny bikini was stretched out on a blanket. Ari could
smell the sweet, coconut odor of her suntan lotion
wafting on the light breeze.

"Mmm. Too bad this all has to come to an end,"
Wendy commented.

"Well, I guess school has to start sometime." Ari laughed. "Actually, I'm pretty psyched. I mean, when I was picking out my classes I sort of felt like the course catalog was this dessert menu and I wanted to try everything. I really couldn't narrow it down. Know what I mean?"

Wendy shrugged. "I guess," she said. "But I'm having a pretty good time just the way it is." She turned her face up to catch the rays, as if she were catching the last bit of summer vacation.

"Wend, there's a reason they call it school," Ari said lightly.

"Yeah? And I thought I was here to socialize," Wendy said. "Speaking of which, a bunch of us are going out dancing tonight. Last hurrah before classes."

Ari thought about Andy and shook her head. "I don't know, Wendy."

"What do you mean, you don't know? It's going to be great. There's this place over in Orangeburg. It was a barn, but they converted it into a restaurant and club. Live band. Dance floor. Bill borrowed his brother's Jeep."

Ari felt torn. Which was starting to be the usual state of affairs. Human rope in a tug-of-war. Andy or the gang? The gang or Andy? Orientation had lasted a week, but somehow Ari felt as if she'd been navigating these strange waters for a lot longer.

"Come on, Ari. You don't really want to stay home alone," Wendy coaxed.

Ari remained silent. What could she say? I won't be alone? I'll be home with my boyfriend the ghost?

"I worry about you," Wendy said. "I hate to think of you by yourself, brooding."

"I won't be brooding," Ari said truthfully. She

78

took a sip of the iced tea she'd bought at the snack bar.

"You could ask that guy," Wendy suggested.

Ari felt herself tighten up. "What guy?" she asked, but she knew full well who Wendy was talking about.

"You know. The guitar guy from the picnic. Bob. The one we saw on our way to dinner the other night."

"Ben," Ari said. They'd run into him and his roommate, Todd, on the way to the dining hall. Ben was looking extra-cute in a pair of faded jeans, a softly worn black T-shirt, and a pair of purple high-tops. He'd greeted her warmly. "Hey, Ari! How're you doing? You met Todd?" Introductions were made all around.

"You guys going to dinner?" Ari had asked. "You don't eat at East, do you?" She'd never seen him there. And if she'd been forced to admit it, she'd say she'd looked.

Ben shook his head. "Took a tip from my big sister and signed up for a food co-op. Barstow—that building that looks like a sand castle over past South Campus?" Ari had noticed it. Stone building with turrets and circular rooms and peculiar decorations. Ben was right. It did look like a sand castle.

"We all take turns doing the shopping and the cooking and the cleaning. Mom would be so proud," he said. "Although, actually, my dad does most of that stuff in our house."

"Sounds cool," Ari said. "You probably get a better meal that way."

Ben arched an eyebrow. "Depends. We had a wicked burned eggplant parmigiana the other day. But, hey, next Wednesday it's my turn, and we're going to feast."

"Yeah? What are you going to make?" asked Ari. Most of the guys she knew weren't so stellar in the kitchen. Andy was pretty good with things like eggs or grilled cheese, but nothing too fancy.

"I thought maybe cheese ravioli primavera. I make a sauce with fresh tomatoes, peppers, peas, broccoli, basil—whatever's really fresh. Lots of garlic, that's the secret. And a big salad with a mango vinaigrette. And some good bread."

Ari's mouth watered. The food co-op sounded like the way to go. At least, when Ben cooked.

"Hey, you guys should be my guests that night," Ben suggested. He was looking straight at Ari as he extended the invitation.

Ari blushed and lowered her gaze. What was she supposed to say? Gee thanks, can I bring my boyfriend? He doesn't eat much. "Maybe," she'd mumbled. "That's really nice of you."

Now, Wendy was waiting for Ari's answer about inviting Ben dancing. Ari frowned and picked at a blade of grass.

"Admit it, girl, you like him," Wendy challenged.

"He's nice," Ari said noncommittally.

"And cute," Wendy persisted.

Ari looked around her. No sign of Andy. At least she didn't see his glimmery form anywhere. "Okay—and cute."

"Then invite him along. If you're too shy, we can get Larry to do it. I saw them talking to each other in the dorm."

Ari groaned. "Larry? I mean, the Lar's a riot and everything, but he'd probably invite the guy and then put a whoopee cushion under his chair. Or under my chair, even worse. Besides . . ." The word hung in the pleasant afternoon air.

Wendy just waited for her to finish her sentence. Ari could feel her roommate's green eyes trained on her.

"I can't," Ari finished. "You just don't understand."

Wendy grew serious. "Okay. You're not ready yet. I do understand, I guess. Or maybe I don't. I've never lost a boyfriend that way. I mean, I'm working on getting one first," she said with a rueful smile.

"You and Mike seem to be hitting it off," Ari said, more than happy to change the subject.

Now it was Wendy's turn to blush. Her fair, freckled face grew as pink as a ripe peach. "We'll see," she said. "But anyway, Ari, at least come with us tonight. Even without the cute guy."

Ari didn't say anything. If Andy hadn't been around, she would have said yes right away. But leave him alone again? To the mercies of the guys in the quad?

"You like to dance, right?" Wendy asked.

Ari nodded. She thought about graduation night— the good part of it, before the accident. Dancing with Andy under the night sky on the deck of the Holiday Inn. Feeling the music vibrating through her. The way Andy had drawn her close when the music slowed down. His powerful grace. His scent. His tender kisses.

"Join the party, Ar," Wendy said softly. "You're so off in your own world sometimes. You've got to go on with your life. Andy would want you to, wouldn't he?"

"Andy loved to dance," Ari said with a sigh. Wait a minute. Loved? Andy loves to dance, she corrected herself silently. Suddenly her mood brightened. "Okay, Wendy. Sure, count me in." Maybe she *would* invite a guy along. The cutest guy. The guy she loved.

"I don't know if it's such a great idea, Ari," Andy was saying. They were spending the afternoon exploring the hiking trails of the nearby state park, following a wooded path up a mountain, the way they used to do so often at home. They were sheltered from the sun by leafy shade, soft pine needles and occasional patches of moss carpeting the path under their feet. It was a secluded spot, and they had chosen it with that in mind.

"You know, it can get kind of weird when you're with other people and I'm around, too." Andy was stating the facts and they both knew it.

"I don't care," Ari said. "If it means we'll be together . . . This place is off campus. It's supposed to be really cool. Wendy says some pretty big bands started out playing there."

"So, go," Andy encouraged. "You definitely should. I just don't want to get in your way, is all."

Ari shrugged. "Then I'd rather just stick around the dorm with you. Wendy'll be out. We'll have all the privacy we want." She tried to sound convincing, but there was a part of her that really did want to go out. She and Andy used to have a total blast hanging out with their friends from high school. And it *was* the last day before classes, after all. The old Andy would have been the first one up and dancing.

Andy seemed to be studying her. "L.M., you didn't come here to hide in your room," he observed. "I think you should go. I really do. Go forth and dance," he commanded in a joking voice. But Ari didn't feel much like laughing.

"Do you want me to leave you alone? Is that it?" Ari's voice was a mixture of irritation and hurt. Maybe Andy was tired of her. Maybe it was boring to spend all his time tagging after her.

"Ari, don't you know I just want you to be happy?" Andy said quietly.

"Then come out with me," Ari said. "Come out with *us*, okay?"

"Look, you weren't that into it when I popped in on you and that Ben guy the day you were registering for classes," Andy said.

Ben, again. Arianne felt herself grow defensive. "That's because I didn't know you were there. This is different. I'm inviting you. I want you to get to know my new friends."

"Yeah?" Andy asked. The path opened up into a little clearing. They walked out into the sun, but Ari noticed that a patch of shade hovered around them. Outdoors or in the dorm room, Andy seemed to be more comfortable sheltered from the light. But Ari had decided it was a minor inconvenience. A little like living with someone who didn't pick up his clothes. Or her clothes, as happened to be the case with a certain fabulous but sloppy roommate.

"Of course I want you to come," she said to Andy. She thought about the way he'd coached her through her first workout the other day. And the jokes he whispered in her ear. The secure feeling of knowing he was there when she needed him. She thought of all the wonderful times they'd shared. Of course she wanted Andy to come with her.

"Well, if you're really sure," he said uncertainly.

Ari smiled. "I mean, unless you'd rather spend another evening with those charming guys from the quad. Listening to them talk about girls when you actually could be with one—who loves you."

She felt her mood warm as his handsome face stretched into the familiar grin. "Well, when you put it that way, okay, I'm sold." Andy did a funny little jig right in the middle of the clearing. His sneakered feet seemed to float right over the rocks and tree roots poking out of the ground. "I'm putting on my dancing shoes . . ."

twelve

Ɗ

Sardines in a can. There were eight of them packed into the borrowed Jeep, with Bill driving. Well, nine, actually, but only Ari and Andy knew that. It was the same crowd who'd hit the campus hot spots a few nights back, minus Marla, who'd already snagged a significant other and was enjoying a more intimate evening, and Cesar, who was out with some of his soccer buddies. Wendy was looking pretty cozy on Mike's lap. Leslie was squeezed against one of the doors but still managed to look totally put together in an ankle-length, flower-print dress. Up front, Shelly and Corinne shared the passenger seat. Ari was balanced on Larry's lap, and Andy in hers.

"An Ari sandwich," Andy whispered in her ear. "Yum, yum. A little honey mustard here ..." He planted an electric kiss on the soft curve of her neck. "A slice of tomato there ..." She felt a tingly little nibble on the other side.

Ari giggled out loud. Fortunately, it wasn't out of place. Every time they took a sharp turn, they all bounced off each other like heated-up atoms. Laughter poured out of the open top of the vehicle.

The latest Squeegies album was blasting from the CD player, and they sang along: "Never get over the blue sky in your eyes . . ."

"Never," sang Larry right to Leslie, "get over the fruit pie in your eyes . . ." He had worn his Cat in the Hat hat for the occasion.

Leslie made her weirdest face at him.

Night was coming. The rolling hills that ringed the university were turning deep purple-gray. The sky was a midnight blue dotted with a few of the first twinkling stars. The summer was giving way to the cool, faintly spicy scent of early fall, and Ari felt that new things were about to happen.

Bill turned up a smaller road, and the Music Barn loomed into view. It really was an old barn, though the red paint and white trim were bright and new, and the windows and big barn doors were edged with strings of lights. Instead of fields and pasture, there was a large parking lot packed with cars. It was definitely the happening spot. As they pulled in, Ari could hear the music pouring out of the club.

They all piled out, stretching cramped arms and legs. Leslie smoothed her long, sleeveless dress. Larry tugged on his hat. Andy linked his arm through Ari's as they headed across the lot toward the music.

Ari felt a rush of exhilaration. Andy's touch felt warm and tingly, and there was something exciting— bordering on forbidden—about having a secret date right out in public. Ari gave Andy's arm a squeeze and flashed him a huge smile.

As they got up to the entrance, they noticed that the lights on the strings were in the shapes of pigs and cows and tiny ears of corn. Inside, the wait staff bustled around in overalls, carrying heaping plates of food and drinks. The chairs were of a rustic, heavy wood. Red-and-white-checked tablecloths covered the tables and sawdust sprinkled the floors.

The music, however, was strictly rock and roll. The band was playing at the rear of the restaurant. Bright, electric sounds filled the room and flooded the dance area in front of the musicians. A handful of people were already up and boogeying. Ari automatically started moving to the rhythms.

The hostess approached them, her long, blond hair flowing out from underneath a blue cap. Her overall shorts had the words "Music Barn" embroidered on the bib. "Hi, all. You're how many this evening?"

"Eight," Shelly answered.

"Nine," Andy said simultaneously.

The hostess nodded and smiled. "How about the hayloft?" She gestured to the upstairs dining area that spanned one side of the cavernous room and opened out onto the rest of the restaurant.

They tromped up the narrow, ladderlike stairs at the side of the loft, and the hostess seated them at her largest table, right next to the railing, overlooking all the action downstairs.

"Great! Front and center," Mike commented. Ari noticed that he scrambled for the seat next to Wendy. Ari took the seat on the other side of her.

"Everyone set?" the hostess asked, handing out menus.

"Well, actually, I told you we were nine," Andy said. "But it's okay. I'll share her chair. I don't mind snuggling." He slipped in next to Ari, and she felt him nuzzling her neck again.

"Andy!" she said under her breath. "You're tickling me."

"Huh? Wendy asked.

"Um, I said I'm tickled by this place," Ari improvised.

"Tickled?" Wendy asked, shooting her a look. "I guess that's one way to put it."

The hostess lit a plain white candle at each end of the long, rectangular table. "Enjoy," she said, leaving them to peruse their menus.

Ari studied the choices. Basics like burgers, barbecued chicken, and ribs. A few fancier dishes like a braised duck and a coconut chicken. A farm salad of different seasonal vegetables, locally made cheese, and a whole-grain breadbasket. Farm salad was definitely the way to go, Ari thought.

"Mmm, everything sounds great. I'm starved," Shelly said. "It's between the ribs and the pasta with garlic sauce."

"I'm a burger and fries man myself," Bill said.

Corinne furrowed her forehead. "What is this cole slaw?" She pronounced it "slaow," to rhyme with "wow." They all tried to fill her in on the finer points of American dining.

"Whatever you get, it'll be *bon appétit* compared to the dining hall," Mike joked.

Ari felt Andy shifting restlessly. "Be back in a sec," he told her. "I'm just going to go check things out." He seemed to vanish. Ari felt a trill of alarm. Then she spotted him wandering around between the tables downstairs and poking his head into the kitchen before going over to stand at the side of the dance floor and listen to the band. But it didn't entirely allay her concern. Was he just going to take off whenever the conversation landed on something that wasn't his speed? Okay, it had to be difficult to be in his shimmery shoes. But it was hard on Ari, too. She thought he should try, at least for her sake.

Across the table, Larry was reading off the menu choices in an overly dramatic way. With his red-and-white-striped hat and the red-and-white tablecloth, Ari wondered if he wasn't just going to suck on a candy cane instead of having dinner. "Tough call," he mused. "Any suggestions?"

Ari heard Andy's voice in her head. "Fish special that's not on the menu. Looks really simple and fresh. Served with mashed potatoes." Then there he was, sliding back in next to Ari.

"There's a special," Ari started to repeat, then snapped her mouth shut. She had to be more careful. But it was too late. Everyone was looking at her. Her pause was measured by the music floating up to the exposed rafters of the hayloft. "Fish and potatoes that look really good," she finished weakly. "I, um . . ."

"Saw someone downstairs eating it when we were on the way in," Andy suggested.

". . . saw someone eating it on the way in when we were downstairs," Ari said. "I mean, we were on the way in. They were downstairs."

Everyone was giving her strange looks. "Yeah," Larry said. "Okay, Ari."

"Oops," said Andy. "I was just trying to help."

Ari nodded ever so slightly and patted Andy's leg. But she couldn't keep out the disloyal thought that she wouldn't have gotten herself into this kind of jam if she'd invited Ben instead. She tried to push the thought out of her head.

A waiter came up the steep stairs, impressively balancing several plates of food. He set them down for the people a few tables away, then whipped an order pad out of his apron and came over to their table.

"How are you all doing tonight?" he asked. A chorus of "Good," rose from the table. "CNE?" he said without waiting for an answer. "Freshmen, right? Just graduated last year, myself. You'll love it here. I do, that's why I decided to stick around."

"Do we have signs across our foreheads that say 'new' or something?" Leslie asked flirtatiously.

The waiter laughed. "Just had a feeling. Besides, I haven't seen any of you around before. So, we have a few specials tonight. For the appetizer, a quesadilla with roasted red peppers; for the entrée, a lake trout served with a spicy orange relish, mashed potatoes, and broccoli. It's really good. The fish is local. Nice and fresh."

Ari lowered her gaze and traced a square on the tablecloth. She could feel everyone look at her as if she had eerie psychic powers.

It got even weirder when their dinner arrived. The whole gang dove into their food as if they hadn't eaten in a week. All right, as if they'd been eating in a dining hall for a week. And Andy hanging out on the edge of Ari's chair, abstaining. She took a little bite of her salad. It was good, but she could barely taste it. She felt like she was trying to be in two places at once.

Finally, Andy got up and started moving around the table. He checked out Corinne's plate. "Le cheeseburger. Solid American choice," he said approvingly. He moved on to Wendy and Mike. "Appetite only for each other," he observed. It was true that they had managed to scoot their chairs awfully close to each other. "You know their legs are touching under the table?" Andy asked.

Ari arched an eyebrow at him. She felt a sizzle of interest at the piece of secret information, but at the same time, she felt as if it really wasn't any of Andy's business.

90

Next, Andy worked his way around to Larry's spot at the table. "And you, my fine feline friend . . ." He sat down right in Larry's lap. Blissfully unaware, Larry was piling his french fries into a kind of pyramid, carefully balancing each one before letting his fingers go. Andy mimicked his every move, stacking the fries, stopping to adjust his hat, sticking the tip of his tongue out in concentration as the pyramid got higher.

And Ari had to admit Andy did a first-rate imitation. She let out a giggle. Andy made his gestures even more exaggerated. She couldn't hold back a loud laugh.

Wendy turned away from Mike just long enough to give Ari a long look. "Well, he's funny," Ari said, pointing in Larry's direction, but really pointing at Andy.

"He is?" Wendy said. Ari could see that her roommate was really starting to wonder about her. She was mildly relieved when Andy quit putting on a show and came back to sit by her side.

As they finished their meals, Andy reached a glowy hand toward the candle at their end of the table. Ari saw his fingers hover above the flame. The light around it dimmed. Sunlight, candlelight—there was that light trick again. He pulled his hand back and the flame burned bright. Ari glanced around covertly. Fortunately, it didn't look as if anyone had noticed. But then he reached out again. The light pulsed. And again. She realized he was playing the flame in time with the drumbeat.

"Oh, my god," Larry murmured. He was looking right at the candle.

Ari shot Andy a warning look, and he stopped.

"That candle!" Larry said. "The flame was moving in time to the music!"

There was a collective moan of, "Oh, Lar!"

"What'd they put in your soda, dude?" asked Mike.

Ari gave Andy a hard pinch. Her fingers went right through him, but he seemed to feel it. "Ouch! L.M., I was just trying to have some fun."

"No, I swear, it was groovin' to the music," Larry insisted. No one took him seriously.

"Speaking of groovin' to the music, anyone want to go down and dance?" Shelly suggested. Ari looked over the balcony. The action on the dance floor was heating up. The little area in front of the band was hopping with bodies in motion.

"Cool!" Ari said enthusiastically. A change in scenery was an excellent idea. The band went into a cover of "Honky Tonk Woman," one of her and Andy's favorite old tunes. It had to be a good sign.

Down on the dance floor, they clustered together in a loose circle. Ari let the beat get into her body. Andy danced next to her. Ari felt the tension draining away. She knew his style, loved his fluid yet inventive way of moving. She worked her arms and gyrated her hips. Andy sang out a line of the song. Ari joined in. A smile stretched across her face. A genuine one.

"You go, girl!" Wendy shouted over the music. Wendy was all over the floor, spinning, jumping, carving patterns with her body. She sashayed over to Ari and bumped her with her hip. Ari bumped back.

The dance floor grew more crowded. People packed the area just in front of the band, overflowing to the aisles around the tables. Ari's little cluster of Eakens pals was broken up by people squeezing out a bit of dance space for themselves. Wendy and Mike split off from the others. Leslie got stuck dancing with the Lar, although Ari was surprised to see that he was a good dancer. Shelly and Corinne were spinning around in the center of the floor. Ari found herself dancing with Bill. And Andy. At the same time.

Bill grinned and did a funny kind of shuffle to the music, waving his arms over his head like swaying wheat. Ari waved her hands back. Andy stepped directly between them and waved, too. It was a little disconcerting. Bill thought he was dancing with Ari. But Ari was face-to-face with Andy. Ari stepped around a little, so that she was facing both of them. It felt more natural to be able to see both her partners clearly. More polite. Andy stepped back between her and Bill again. Ari stepped around once more. Andy did, too. Was Andy jealous?

Bill just sort of rotated on his axis, a mildly bewildered expression on his big, rectangular face as he followed Ari's orbit. Ari felt her frustration rising. Maybe dancing hadn't been the best idea. She was glad when the band hit the final chords of the song. But her relief was short-lived, as they went into a slow number and the lights over the dance floor grew dim. Ari saw Wendy melt into Mike's arms, her eyes closing, a smile on her lips. She felt Bill looking at her. Andy, too. Her face grew hot.

She thought about how she and Andy used to dance together, her body following his so easily and naturally, his warmth, his grace, the feel of his heart beating . . .

Bill took a tentative step toward her. Ari felt her breath catch in her throat. She looked at Andy. But he was suddenly looking intently at the stage, as if the band and their equipment were the only things in the room. And all of a sudden there was a loud popping noise from that direction. The amp let off an explosive sound and died. The guitarist strummed, the drummer's sticks tapped out a beat, but the music no longer poured from the speakers. The musicians put down their instruments. The bass player went over to the control box and started fiddling with the knobs and dials.

A groan went up from the crowd. But Andy was grinning. Ari had a flash of realization. A computer, a stereo, an electric amp . . . This was no accident! Ari saw Wendy and Mike let go of each other, shy disappointment on their faces. Ari's anger rose in her throat.

"Bill, will you excuse me for a few minutes? I need to get a little fresh air." She gestured to Andy and led him toward the door. She didn't stop until they were outside and in back of the barn, alone.

"What exactly were you trying to do in there?" she yelled, not even attempting to keep her voice down.

Andy put his hands up. "Whoa, Ari. Hold on. You mean you wanted to dance with that guy?" Andy began miming Bill's shuffling, wheat-waving moves.

"That's not funny, Andy! And no, I didn't want to dance with him. I mean, not slow dance with him. But you had no right to pull the plug on everyone else's night."

Andy's handsome face creased into a frown. "Seems to me you were looking pretty uncomfortable when that slow song came on. Seems to me I did you a favor in there."

"I was uncomfortable? More like *you* were uncomfortable. More like you can't stand for me to even talk to anyone else."

"Is that right?" Andy yelled back.

"Yeah. I wanted you to get to know my friends and all you're doing is making fun of them."

"Hey, I was just trying to have a little fun. I thought that's what you wanted. For us to go out with your friends and have a good time."

"Except that you're acting like a total jerk." Ari felt herself snap. "What's the matter with you, Andy? Just because you're not the life of the party anymore?" She regretted it the second the words were out of her mouth.

Andy's expression grew dark and unhappy. "That was a low blow," he said softly. "No, I'm not the life of the party. I'm the death."

Arianne felt all the fight go out of her, like air escaping from a balloon. Tears stung her eyes. "I'm sorry, Andy. I'm really sorry."

"Look," he said, "how about we both agree that this wasn't the smartest idea." Ari nodded through her tears. "I never wanted to make you sad. Never. Just the opposite, L.M. Totally the opposite." She felt his soft, electric kiss on her cheek. "You have fun with your friends and I'll meet you back at the dorm later."

When Wendy came and found her, she was standing behind the Music Barn, crying. Alone.

thirteen

Andy floated up over the Music Barn, in no hurry to get back to campus. From where he hung in the sky, the bustling night spot looked like a piece from a child's game, the strings of lights twinkling like holiday decorations. The evening was peaceful, the landscape dark and mountainous, dotted with houses, their windows aglow. He could see the whole panorama at once—the town nestled in the valley; the stretches of woods and fields; the CNE campus; the brook that ran behind South Quad and opened into a river farther downstream. He was in all those places at once, listening to the rush of cold water as the river flowed over loose rocks, to a mother sing her child to sleep, to the raucous music of a party back at school. But the thrill had worn off. He was tired. Or would have been if he got tired anymore. He couldn't even count on the release of sleep. He couldn't bear leaving Ari crying by herself, but they both knew it would have gotten worse had he stayed.

He let himself float up farther. He searched for the warm, brilliant light he was used to feeling above him, the comforting light somewhere above a night that was no longer his. It was there; he could feel it and see the edge of brilliance splitting the velvet black sky. But tonight it was distant, more distant than it had ever been before, and the lure of pure joy seemed hopelessly out of reach.

Don't lose your way . . . He remembered the words that had echoed in his head. Was it slipping away from him? The place where he could feel he belonged? He grabbed for the rays of light and peace and let himself drift toward them.

But down—way, way down—below him, he could feel Ari's sadness. No. Not yet. He forced himself to let go of the light. He shut the blissful sensations out of his mind. He brought his attention back down to earth and he could feel a wave of heaviness descending on him as he did.

Don't lose your way . . . But Ari was his way. And Ari needed him. He trained his focus on the Music Barn again. The bass player had gotten the amp fixed. The music was pumping again. Wendy and Mike were back on the dance floor, rocking out. The others were talking and laughing over dessert up in the hayloft. But Ari sat quietly in her seat, looking sad, barely touching her chocolate cake. So beautiful, but so unhappy. Andy's heart nearly broke in two.

No, he just couldn't leave her like this.

"Admit it. I was right. It was a terrible idea for me to come with you," Andy said to her. They sat on the edge of her bed, with several inches of uncomfortable distance between them. Wendy was still out with Mike, taking a moonlit walk somewhere. Right this second, Arianne could barely remember when it had been that new and romantic for her and Andy.

97

"Fine. I admit it," Ari said. "I'm sorry I dragged you along."

The silence swelled between them. Ari swallowed hard. Her new friends were hungrily taking in their new town, their new school, their new experiences. Wendy was just getting to know a brand-new, wonderful guy. Ari felt a sting of jealousy. She remembered what Loren had told her, so many months earlier. That college was for new things, new boys. Maybe Loren was right.

An image of Ben pushed its way into her mind. Ben in his purple high-tops. Ben, deciding to be majorly undecided because there was still too much he hadn't tried.

Andy had it all planned out. Or he had, before . . . A schedule of premed courses, the sciences, math. A shelf of swimming trophies. A good med school, one with a sports medicine program he could follow. After his internship, he'd move back to Portwater. Open his own practice. Build a beautiful house for him and Ari, start a family.

It had seemed like the perfect plan to Ari, too. She'd act in the Portwater regional theater, maybe try her hand at directing. Teach theater in the local schools. But now she was beginning to wonder how a person could be so sure, without even exploring other possibilities. She put her head in her hands and sighed. Portwater was a beautiful town, but it wasn't the only place in the world.

Andy broke the silence. "Any time you want, I'll leave."

Arianne didn't answer for a long time. She tried to imagine it, imagine every day without Andy's voice. To never hear it, ever again? Never hear him cheer her on for just one more lap, a little more, a little faster? Never hear him crack another joke? Never feel the love in his electric touch? She raised her head and looked up at him with moist eyes. In the near darkness, his face shone, and he looked more handsome than ever. She'd counted on him for so long. Without him this summer, she'd barely felt alive.

She moved toward him and put her arms around him. She felt the soft sting of electricity describing the lean, muscular form of the body she knew so well. Tentatively, he returned her hug. She let herself melt into his arms. She felt so safe with him, so secure. "Don't go, Andy," she whispered. "Please don't go."

"But, L.M., I don't want to be holding you back. You're meeting all these new people, making new friends."

She shook her head. "A couple of weeks ago I didn't even know them. Andy, you're the one I've always wanted to be with." And as she said it, she thought about how true that was. Ever since she'd met him, she only wanted to be with Andy. Without him, a party wasn't nearly as fun, a sunset wasn't nearly as beautiful, a song not nearly as good. "This is how I always wanted it to be. Me and you. The two of us. Remember?"

He nodded. "Eternally yours." She felt him kiss the top of her head. Then her forehead, her brow, the tip of her nose. She brought her lips up to meet his. His kiss was charged with love and passion.

Ari responded tentatively at first. Then her body and emotions took over. She kissed him more deeply. She felt a wave of love. This was Andy, her Andy. They caressed each other gently, each part of her body thrilling to his electric touch. The feather-light graze of his fingers seemed to be everywhere at once, letting loose multiple currents of pleasure. She felt every part of her come alive. Time seemed to slip away. There was only the sensation, the moment. She shivered with delight. As if in a kind of dream, she lay back and abandoned herself to Andy's indescribable touch.

"Ari! Ari! You gotta wake up!" Wendy's voice made its way through a deep fog of sleep, and Ari felt her roommate shaking her by the shoulders.

She opened one eye. "Jeez, Wendy, what's up?"

"Well, not you. Come on, first day of classes and we both overslept!" Wendy grabbed a pair of black jeans from the floor and pulled them on as she talked. "If you don't hurry up, you're going to be late." She pulled a white V-necked T-shirt over her head.

Late on the first day? Ari was suddenly wide awake. "Whoa! What happened? What time is it anyway?" She was on her feet in a flash.

Wendy shrugged. "That clock hasn't really worked right since we got here. Plus the late night and all . . ." Wendy slowed down for a second as a dreamy smile crept across her face.

Ari remembered her own romantic night. Andy's kisses, their closeness. She glanced around the room, but she didn't see him. The thrilling memory of his touch, however, was fresh in her mind. "Great night, huh?" she said to Wendy.

"Totally," Wendy agreed, in motion again as she hastily stuffed her feet into her basketball shoes. Suddenly, she stopped in mid-action. She fixed Ari with a confused stare. "It was? I mean it was for *me* . . ."

Ari just laughed. "You and Mike? Details, girl-friend. I want to hear the details."

Wendy giggled. "Oh, Ari, we had the best time. We took this incredible walk under the stars . . ." Then she glanced at her watch as she strapped it on her slender, freckled wrist. "But I'll have to tell you all about it later. First class is in Wilde, all the way on the other end of campus. Meet me back here before dinner tonight?"

"Uh-huh." Ari nodded, but Wendy had already grabbed her stuff and was out the door.

Ari pulled on her blue silk bathrobe, the one Andy had given her on the anniversary of their first kiss. Their first kiss, tasting of popcorn, in one of the back rows of the Cineplex, neither of them paying any attention to the thriller on the screen.

Where was Andy anyway? Ari wriggled into her slippers and grabbed her soap, toothpaste, and toothbrush. She let herself out of the room, making sure the door was unlocked, and headed toward the women's bathroom.

And just as she passed the quad, there he was. Andy, floating through the quad door and into the hall. Ari stopped. He looked at her and smiled. "Morning, L.M. How'd you sleep?"

His hair was rumpled and his shoes were untied. His eyes were on the puffy side. It looked like he had had a wild night. Ari thought she caught a whiff of alcohol emanating from under the door to the quad. And a breath of something sickly sweet mixed in. She thought it might be marijuana. "Andy, what have you been doing in there?" Andy had never needed any liquor or drugs to make life more fun.

"Doing? Not much. Just hanging out," said Andy. "Passing the wee hours with the guys, you know?"

"No, I don't know," Ari replied severely. "It smells like you've been getting into all kinds of stuff in there."

"*Moi?*" Andy said with exaggerated innocence. "Look, okay, Ari, the boys are kind of into getting fried. But, hey, I don't even do lunch or dinner anymore. Let alone the harder stuff." He laughed. Ari didn't.

"I thought you thought those guys were jerks."

Andy made a sheepish face. "I do. But they're the only ones who like my tricks."

"Your tricks?"

"Yeah, playing around with the stereo, doing that candle thing that you hated so much at the Music Barn. Actually, I did it with their cigarette lighter. But you know, stuff like that."

"Andy, I didn't hate that candle thing," Ari protested. "Actually, it was pretty cool. I just didn't want you doing it in front of everyone else," she said. "I mean, what did you expect them to think? What do those meatheads in there think, anyway?"

Andy gave a little shrug and laughed. "They don't think. At least, not that much. I don't know. They can sense something, sense my presence in some spaced-out sort of way. Sean, the one who looks like a wasted surfer? The one Wendy thought was a babe? He actually saw me sitting on his bed for a minute. 'Whoa, check it out, bros. We got some pretty weird company,'" Andy imitated. "'Course they all just thought he'd been getting too messed up."

"Andy, you know I don't like you hanging out with those kinds of people. And for your information, Wendy only thought Sean was a babe *before* she found out what a moron he is."

Andy groaned. "Don't you think I know that, Ari? Look, it's just a way to get me through the night. Besides, their whole goal is basically to blast themselves into another world by whatever means possible.

And they almost manage to do it. Which kind of gives them something in common with me. And they appreciate me, okay?'' he added pointedly.

Arianne blew out a long, noisy breath. "Andy, I appreciate you. Didn't I make that pretty clear last night?''

Andy seemed to loose his defensive edge. "Yeah, hey, that was really wonderful,'' he said.

"For me, too." Ari could feel herself starting to blush. "Listen, I'm just a little worried about you, spending time in there.'' She gestured with her head toward the door of the quad.

"Worried? Ari, what could possibly happen to me?''

Ari thought about it for a second. She could see his point. But she felt as if he'd missed *her* point entirely.

Andy didn't pick up on her frustration. "I did my clock trick for them when they were really out of it. Made the numbers go backwards, and then forwards and backwards again. They got into this pretty whacked-out discussion about how time had no meaning. Oo-ee-ooo. But that's basically how it is for me, so in some twisted way they were on my wavelength.''

Ari held back from rolling her eyes. "Look, speaking of clock tricks, you've gotta stop messing with our clock. The alarm didn't go off this morning, and I'm really late. In fact, I have to hustle or I'm going to be late to my first college class ever.'' She felt a sense of urgency come over her. "I think I missed breakfast already.''

"Yeah, okay, L.M. Go get ready,'' Andy said. "I'll walk you to class.''

Ari nodded. It was nice of him to offer. But deep down, she kind of wished he would let her walk to class by herself.

fourteen
𝒟

"*So, what'd you think?*" Ben waited for Ari to put her notebook in her backpack, and they walked out of their first class on the first day of their first semester of college together.

"I think the reading list is immense," Ari said. "Did Professor Greenburg leave one single myth from one tiny little forgotten culture off that list?"

"It's of mythic proportions, one might say?"

Ari laughed. "One might. I definitely would. My high school was pretty rigorous, especially the A.P. classes. But we probably would have taken the whole year to read all the stuff on this list, not one semester."

They paused outside the classroom door. The second floor of Whitney, the main classroom building for humanities, sported floor-to-ceiling windows that looked out on Central Bowl. Ari could see students hurrying from class to class, to the library, to the mail room, criss-crossing the narrow cement walkways and the grassy bowl itself. In the hall of Whitney, kids consulted their class schedules, read the numbers over the doors, wasted a few minutes between classes.

"No one's going to read every single one of those books anyway," Ben commented with a shake of his dark, curly-haired head. "After dealing with the guy today, I'm sure it's part of Greenburg's macho act. You know, like some kind of classroom bravado. My class is bigger and tougher than all the other classes."

Ari arched an eyebrow. "Well, you definitely are taking him on already. I think he was a little shocked."

Professor Greenburg was short and dumpy, with rumpled slacks and his thick glasses askew. But inside the little man lived the soul of a football coach. "MYTH," he'd written on the board in bold capitals, without a single word of preamble or introduction to the class. Then he'd spun around to issue a challenge. "Define it. Someone. You, there, with the yellow dress and blond hair."

The girl in the first row seemed to shrink from his outstretched index finger. "Um, ah, something that isn't true," she said meekly.

"You have on a red dress. That's not true. Is it a myth?"

Ari could see the girl turning pink. But Professor Greenburg was already pointing to his next victim. The boy he chose did a little bit better. "An untrue story about something true."

"Something?" the teacher shot back. "You have to be less vague in my class, people. You. Long black hair, white T-shirt." He was looking right at Ari.

"Ah, a story about forces in the world?" she said unsteadily. "Or people or animals. The way things in the world got the way they are?"

"Rain is formed when moisture condenses into clouds," Professor Greenburg said. "Story about how something in the world got the way it is. Myth?'' He shook his round head.

His game of cat-and-mouse continued until he had pounced on several more students and further honed his definition of *myth*. He scribbled a few more things on the blackboard: "the unknown"; "user-friendly explanation"; "attempt to tame the world."

When he turned back around, Ari could feel everyone in the room holding his or her breath, waiting to see who would be on the spot next. From the back of the room, Ben spoke up. "Isn't that kind of a negative definition?" he asked. He had come in even later than Ari, just as the bell was ringing, and slid into an empty seat at the back of the class. But now he was in the thick of the action. Ari turned to look at him. He *was* pretty cute.

"I mean, your definition suggests that myths arise from fear," Ben said. "Fear of something we don't understand. Seems to me, it's more a matter of respect or celebration. Like an ode to how things came to be and how things are."

"Oh, an ode," Professor Greenburg uttered, lingering on both "o" sounds in a sardonic way. "So you think the tooth fairy is an ode to having a tooth fall out of your mouth? You think that it isn't terribly frightening for a young child to have a part of his body just fall off, Mr. . . . ?"

"Mr. Curtis. Ben Curtis." He seemed to be thoroughly enjoying his face-off with the teacher. "And that's a pretty gruesome description of loosing a tooth. But the tooth fairy replaces the tooth with a gift or a coin, just like the old tooth is going to be replaced by a new tooth. So, a myth is kind of showing you what's going to happen and making you realize that there *is* something to celebrate, even in loss or change."

Now, standing outside the classroom with Ari, Ben laughed easily. "A guy like that wants you to sock it to him. He's asking for it. He loves it. Although I did feel a little like I was out there in the ring waving a red flag."

"Well, I give you lots of credit," Ari said. "I was just hoping he wouldn't call on me again."

"That's why you have to be the aggressor," Ben said without a trace of aggression. "Tell him what you think before he has a chance to launch some sneaky question at you first."

"I guess," Ari said with a laugh.

"So, what's next on your schedule?" Ben asked.

"Nothing until eleven. That's Human Biology. I was going to go to the snack bar and get something to eat. I slept through breakfast, and I'm totally starved."

"I've got a better idea," Ben said. "I'm off 'till eleven, too. And I discovered that the bakery in town makes these incredible muffins. I mean, if you don't mind my cutting in on your breakfast."

Ari felt her pulse pick up. But then she thought about Andy. She glanced around nervously, as if he might have decided to pay her an unexpected visit.

"Something the matter?" Ben asked.

Ari shook her head. There was no sign of Andy. He'd told her he'd probably be spending the morning popping in on a bunch of different classes. Besides, having a muffin with Ben wasn't exactly a crime. "Sure, that sounds good," she said.

"Great," Ben replied. "Maybe we can stop at the bookstore after and start carting home all the books we have to buy for class."

*　　*　　*

"So, you looked like you were actually having fun getting in the ring and waving that red flag," Ari commented to Ben, continuing their earlier conversation.

They sat on a green painted bench outside the bakery, eating muffins and sipping cappuccini. The bakery was on a small side street off the busy main strip, a good spot for a quiet coffee break. Ari hadn't been able to decide between the carrot spice and the blueberry corn, so they'd gotten one of each and were sharing them.

"Olé, olé!" Ben said. "Any matador's gotta feel a rush when he waves that flag and the bull comes at him. Have you ever seen an actual bullfight?"

Ari took a sip of coffee. "No way!" She wrinkled her nose. "Those things are totally barbaric. Talk about cruelty to animals. Anyway, we don't get too many bullfights coming to Portwater," she added with a laugh. "How about you? Have you ever seen one?"

Ben nodded. "My family moved around a lot when I was growing up. We lived in Granada in the south of Spain, for a while. Bullfighting originated in that part of the world. First time I went, I felt exactly like you do." Ben took a big bite of the carrot muffin. "Mmm, good!"

"First time? You mean you went again!? I have to tell you I think that's kind of twisted." Maybe Ben wasn't the sweet, nice guy she'd thought.

"Look, I agree, it's a raw deal for the bull. And basically I think it'd be better if they took up kite flying or something else less brutal as a national pastime. But at the same time, it's this incredible spectacle. Ritual and drama, the power of life and death. I mean, death is a major force in life." Ben gave a little embarrassed laugh. "I guess that sounds pretty flaky, huh?"

Ari thought about Andy, invisibly surfing from class to class somewhere. "I understand what you're saying better than you think."

"You do? Cool. I was afraid you might think I'm some kind of bloodthirsty beast. Foe of animals, stuff like that."

"Well, I think that, too," Ari said sweetly. "And just don't try inviting me to a bullfight."

"Okay," Ben said, laughing. "I'll stick to muffins and coffee. But you know, it's a cultural experience. The Spanish equivalent of, well, maybe baseball and opera put together."

"Except they don't kill the tenor at the end of the opera," Ari pointed out.

"No, but they might try to kill the umpire," Ben said.

"Point to you," Ari conceded. She took one bite of each muffin. "I like the carrot better. How about you?"

"Carrot. Like the walnuts in it."

"I've only been to the opera once," Ari said. "In Boston, actually. *La Bohème*. I didn't get a lot of it, but I really liked the big show—the music and the costumes and the fancy sets and the whole *grandness.*"

"Yeah, that's what I mean about bullfighting," Andy said excitedly.

"Don't push it," Ari said lightly.

"Oh. Okay. So, how about those Red Sox?" Ben joked.

"Now, baseball, there's something I know about," Ari said. "Played shortstop on my Little League team when I was growing up."

"Yeah?" Ben sounded impressed. "Not me. I was the wimpy kid who took music lessons instead. You'd probably have wupped my butt if you'd met me when we were little.''

Ari laughed. Ben was really interesting, even if he could stand a little enlightenment from People for the Ethical Treatment of Animals. Ari couldn't imagine talking to Andy about opera and baseball in the same sentence.

"Last bite?" Ben held the rest of the corn muffin out as an offering.

"Sure. Thanks.'' Ari took it from him and their hands brushed against each other. She felt a tingle. Not the breeze-light electric tingle of Andy's touch, but the solid, warm contact of flesh and muscle and bone. It felt awfully good.

They finished their muffins and coffee, but neither of them made any move to go. "So, what did your parents do that you moved around so much?" Ari asked.

"They're both professors," Ben said. "Between sabbaticals and exchange arrangements with foreign universities, we lived in a lot of places.''

"Wow. That sounds really cool," said Ari. "And it explains a lot," she added pointedly.

"About . . . ?"

"About you and Professor Greenburg. I guess you're more used to standing up to professors than the rest of us are.''

"Well, they're only human," Ben agreed. "So, how do you like living in Eakens so far? You and your roommate look like you're hitting it off pretty well.''

"Yeah, Wendy's great. I really got lucky. A bit of a slob is the only minor problem. But I mean, the interior decorating in those rooms isn't so great in the first place, so I guess it doesn't matter so much.''

"Green," Ben stated as if it meant something.

Ari's brow furrowed a little. "Actually, our curtains and bedspreads are this ugly orange-and-brown pattern."

"No, I meant green as in greenery. Plant life. That's what you need to make those rooms feel more lived in." Ben suddenly got to his feet and took Ari's hand, pulling her up off the bench, too. "Come on!" he said. "Let's go!"

Ari allowed herself to hold his hand a beat longer than was utterly necessary. When she let go, it was with a touch of reluctance. "Go where?" she asked.

"Plant store," answered Ben. "I know exactly the thing and where to get it!"

Ari let Ben lead the way. Somehow, with him, a trip to the plant store felt like an adventure.

"Don't tell me. You cut classes and went on a shopping spree," Wendy said, putting the book she was reading on her bed.

Ari plunked the heavy shopping bags in the middle of the floor, on one of the few bare patches free of Wendy's clothes, shoes, and tattered dance gear. "Nope. I mean, yeah, I did go shopping. But then I lugged these bags around to Human Bio and the dining hall and then to Psych class." She shook her arms out. "I'm gonna feel it, too, when I get in the pool tomorrow. So, where were you at lunch, anyway?" she asked.

Wendy got a dopey, dreamy smile on her face.

"Wait. Let me guess," Ari said. She plopped down on her bed. It felt good to take the weight off her feet. "You and a certain someone skipped lunch."

Wendy looked sheepish. "Guilty as charged. I got something at the snack bar later. So, what'd you buy?"

"That's it?" Ari demanded playfully. "Guilty as charged? That's all you're going to tell me?"

Wendy looked over at Ari. "Well . . ." She wiggled an eyebrow. "Okay, so after the Music Barn we took this awesome walk. It was the perfect night. Perfect temperature, all these stars. We made wishes on them out in the field behind the gym. All this space back there, and just the two of us." Wendy let out a long, soft sigh and seemed to go off into dreamland.

"And?" prompted Ari.

"Oh. And so we talked. At first," Wendy added with a little giggle. "But like, we really talked. Everything from our favorite colors and our middle names to philosophy and the meaning of life."

"Meaning of life, huh?" teased Ari. "Did you figure out the answers to any really big questions?"

Wendy laughed. "Well, we found out that we really get along. Ari, I totally like this guy," she said with more intensity. "Anyway, we were just standing there in the middle of the field, and, well, you know!"

Ari laughed. "Yeah, I guess I do. I guess you got what you wished for on those stars."

"Shh!" Wendy said. "You're not supposed to tell!"

"And lunch today? More 'you know'?" Ari said lightly.

"Ari, I just have to tell you; the guy is the absolute best kisser!"

Ari grinned. "I'm happy for you, Wendy. Really."

"So, now are you going to tell me what you bought?" Wendy asked. She got off her bed and went over to peer into the bags. "Ooh, flowers," she said. "Pretty."

"It's a begonia plant, actually." Ari smiled to herself. Ben had insisted on buying it as a present for her. "The other bag is full of books. All for one class, can you believe it?"

Wendy eyed the oversized, double-bagged shopping bag. "Yeah? None of my classes were that bad. At least, not the ones I had today. What class are they for, anyway?"

"Greenburg. Literature of Myth." Ari kicked off her chunky-soled sandals and let them drop on the floor next to the bed. "The myth is that we'll have time to read them all."

Wendy laughed. "You buy a semester's worth of No-Doz with them?"

"I need it, huh? So how *were* your classes, anyway? Or were you too busy daydreaming about Mike Wonderful to be able to say?"

Wendy grimaced. "Well, now that you mention it . . . No, seriously, they seem good. I mean, I was more into them than I thought I'd be. Intro to Poetry, especially. And I had my first CNE ballet class this afternoon. The studio's really nice. It's over in Parsons, that old building with all the ivy? It's got these beautiful wood floors and tons of light . . . Speaking of which, we've gotta get some more lights for this room. Your side especially. I really don't get it. It seems like it's dark in here even when it should be sunny."

Ari felt a glimmer of discomfort. She knew whose fault that was. "Yeah, well, we could use a lot of things in this room. Some nice stuff on the walls, maybe a rug. Maybe a housekeeper, while we're at it."

Wendy blushed. "I'm going to clean up this weekend. I mean it. And then we can get to work decorating. The plant's a good start, though." She pulled open the handles of the shopping bag for a better look. Tiny, silky red flowers and large, oval, waxy green leaves spilled over the top of the bag. Wendy put her nose to them. "Mmm, nice," she said. "We can use a little life in this room. That's really nice of you. Thanks, Ari."

Life in this room. Life of the party. Death of the party. Wendy didn't have any idea what appropriate words she'd chosen. Ari tried not to dwell on it. Not when she'd had such a good day. "Well, actually, Wend," Ari confessed, "I didn't buy it. It was a present."

"A present? Who from?" Wendy asked, arching an eyebrow.

"A present from Ben," Ari said, feeling her face grow warm as she said his name.

Wendy looked from Ari to the plant and back to Ari. A big smile stretched across her face. "Way to go, girl," she said quietly. And then, as if she just couldn't resist, she added, "See, I knew you guys liked each other. I was right, wasn't I?"

"It's nothing, Wendy." Suddenly Ari wondered if she should have said anything about Ben. "He's just a friend. We had a morning class together, and we went into town to get something to eat. I mean, because I missed breakfast and all. Then we started talking, and we got on the subject of the dorm rooms and I said how I thought . . ." She stopped mid-sentence. "I'm babbling. Sorry."

"Hey, it's okay, Ari." Wendy came over and sat down next to her. "I understand what you're saying. It's fine that he's just a friend." She reached over and

114

gave a lock of Ari's hair a tug. "You know, just a friend is pretty nice."

Ari took a couple of deep breaths. "Yeah, it is nice. Thanks for being so sweet about, well, about everything."

Wendy just nodded. She gave Ari a chance to settle down. "So how were *your* classes?" she asked. "Tell me all about them."

She didn't mention the plant or Ben again. Ari was grateful for Wendy's sensitivity and solid friendship. The mess in the room was an awfully tiny trade-off. Ari knew she couldn't have gotten a better roommate. She just wished she could tell Wendy what was really happening.

"*𝒴ou're quiet tonight,*" Andy observed, lying back on Ari's bed.

Ari was borrowing Wendy's bed, across the room, sitting stiffly on the end of it. The high spirits she'd felt all day had definitely been parked outside the door. She shrugged and said nothing.

"Head spinning from all that new knowledge you picked up today?" Andy joked lightly.

"I guess," Ari said. Her head *was* spinning. But more from confusion than academics. Wendy and Mike were off at the library, studying. Or pretending to. Leslie and some of the others had gone to hear the open-mike poetry reading at the Bean and Bass. Ari was sitting in near darkness.

She'd meant what she'd said the other night, when she'd told Andy that she wanted it to be just the two of them. But right now she was as lonely as she'd ever been. She felt as separate and apart from the rest of the world as she'd felt right after Andy's accident. The rest of them were going ahead with their lives, laughing over bad poetry, waving red flags. And Ari was sitting here yearning for the old days, for the times when she and Andy had been out there living their lives, too.

Ari felt hollow inside. She couldn't go backward and she couldn't go forward. She was nowhere. She hurt. She might as well have been on Cahill Beach again, sitting with her knees pulled up to her chest and staring out at the water. Except at least on the beach she was somewhere beautiful, somewhere she could feel the huge forces that were larger than any one person or her problems, where nature's majesty and raw power dwarfed her pain and the rhythmic crash of the waves soothed her.

"You okay, L.M.? Didn't you have a good day?"

Ari heard the concern in Andy's voice. He cared so much. Yet she couldn't manage to snuff out an ember of resentment. If he hadn't been here, she'd be out having fun.

Having fun? *Get real*, she chastised herself. All summer long, her friends from home had invited her out. Sometimes she'd gone, most of the time she hadn't. But it hadn't made a difference. She'd spent every second with a deep ache in her chest. Her smile had never gone deeper than the surface. And she'd had a miserable time after Andy left the Music Barn the other night. So why couldn't she just be happy to be with him?

"Yeah, I did have a good day," she said, trying to make her voice brighter than she felt. "I told you, I think I'm going to like the classes I've had so far. I mean, if I survive Professor Greenburg and manage to get all the work done."

"You can always switch to Rocks for Jocks," Andy said. "Actually, it was pretty interesting. Today we learned about the different layers of the Earth's surface and how you can read the whole history of the planet in them. Or you could try Physics for Poets. The teacher's nice, and it doesn't seem like he's going to give a lot of work. But stay away from Madame Duffy's French class. I think she's worse than your Professor Greenburg.''

Ari managed a weak smile. ''Thanks, but I think I'll stick with what I've got. You planning on trying out every class at CNE before the semester's through?''

''We call it auditing, L.M. All the info, none of the work. No big tuition bills to pay, either.''

Andy was trying to make her laugh. But Ari just wasn't in a laughing mood. ''Speaking of tuition,'' she said, ''I forgot to tell you that I think I got a campus job three nights a week. Checking IDs over at the gym.''

''Yeah? That's good. Probably a good way to meet people, too,'' Andy said.

Ari felt herself bristle. *I am meeting people*, she thought silently. *The problem is that I can't hang out with them.* She couldn't bring herself to meet Andy's gaze. She let her own gaze roam anywhere but in his direction. The textured white ceilings that looked like they'd been plastered over strands of spaghetti, the bookshelves she'd already started to fill up. The begonia that now had a starring position on her windowsill. Her gaze lingered on it.

''Nice touch,'' Andy said. ''I like the little red flowers.''

Ari felt a flutter of guilt. ''Yeah. Um, thanks. I thought it would brighten up the room. Make it look a little less like Early Motel,'' she tried to joke. Why did she have to feel like such a criminal about Ben? All she'd done was have breakfast with a classmate. Soak up ''the college experience,'' as Andy might have called it. Okay, so Ben had insisted on buying her a little housewarming present. But it wasn't like she'd gone out on a date with him or anything.

Ari stifled a sigh. She wasn't being honest with herself. The truth of the matter was that she wouldn't have minded a date with Ben. But to have Andy leave her, to never, ever see him again—it was too awful to contemplate.

They sat there in silence for a long, long time. Finally, without moving, Andy turned on the radio, softly. The tune was upbeat, some rock and roll classic with about a total of three chords and a catchy rhythm. Andy started singing along.

But Ari couldn't get her mood to lift. "Hey, Andy?"

"Yeah?" He sat up to look at her.

"Would you mind if I went out and took a little walk?"

Andy shook his head. "You need to be alone, L.M.?"

"Maybe just for a little while."

"No problem," he said understandingly. It only made her feel worse. Andy was so sweet, so caring, so there for her. She didn't deserve him being so nice to her.

She grabbed a light sweater and made a dash for the door. She didn't know what she wanted anymore.

Andy watched the door close between him and Ari. Where was the vibrant person he knew and loved? The one who let loose and danced under the stars with him? The one who always tried to be in front when they went out mountain biking? The one who loved his jokes? Ari seemed so subdued, so sad. Andy felt his own mood sinking at least as low as hers. He was working harder and harder to try to coax a smile from her. And it was working less and less. Without her in the room, he could just give up and give in to bleakness.

He was too sad to do much of anything. He shifted listlessly on Ari's bed. He fiddled with the radio, but he couldn't find anything he was in the mood to listen to. He switched the radio off and lay in the dark. Maybe a game of "Lost Treasure"? Nah, he'd probably get nailed by the enemy tonight. Besides, what was he going to do? Play computer games for all of eternity?

He barely had the energy to lift his weightless body off the bed. He didn't know what he could do to make Ari smile again, really smile, so that he could see some essential spark of her in her happy expression. He'd moved heaven and earth to be with her to make her happy. And it wasn't working. What else could he do?

He cast his glance around Ari's and Wendy's room. He didn't have the will to travel any farther. Tonight he couldn't feel even a ray of the joyous bright light, so why bother going anywhere at all? A pair of Wendy's shorts were draped over the back of a stiff, wooden chair; a pile of Ari's books were on the bare floor next to the bed. Ari was right. The room *was* furnished in Early Motel.

Held hostage in a cheap motel room for eternity. Maybe when he died, he'd actually gone the other way. He gave a small, hard laugh. Well, the room would look nicer with some personal touches. Ari and Wendy just needed to get around to that decorating they'd been threatening to do—buying a rug, putting up some posters. And the strapping begonia was certainly a start.

The begonia. Andy felt a tug of hurt. Ari would be furious if she knew he'd been watching when she and that Ben guy had bought it. Andy had only popped in on her for a second. He'd wanted to see how her day was going, tell her about the lecture in Rocks for Jocks. But he'd realized right away that he hadn't picked the greatest time for a visit. He fixed the plant with a hostile stare, as if it was the source of his troubles. Yeah, Ari would kill him if she found out.

Suddenly, Andy let out a loud, bitter laugh. Wait a minute. Kill him? That would be a little difficult to do.

He floated up off the bed and right through the door. He figured he might as well go down to the quad and see what those stoners were up to.

Ari took a breath of cool night air. Somewhere nearby, someone had built the first fire of the season in a fireplace. Ari could smell the distinctive smoky note on the light breeze. Tonight only the brightest stars were visible, shining diamond-sharp in the blue-black sky. Sometimes Ari liked it better this way. Without a haze of too many stars, the strongest ones stood out even more clearly, forming the patterns of the constellations.

Almost automatically, Ari found the Big Dipper. And there was Orion's Belt, with the sword hanging down. And there were the seven sisters, even though there were only six stars in that cluster.

Ari gave a short, sharp laugh. Maybe the seventh one was a ghost. Actually, she didn't find too much humor in that tonight. Nor was she much in the mood

for stargazing. She crossed the stretch of grass between Eakens and the gym, and followed the path
around the huge, modern, steel-and-glass building to
the athletic field behind it.

It was the same route Wendy and Mike had taken
on their famous moonlit walk. Ari felt a sizzle of jealousy. Wendy was just throwing herself headlong into
whatever was going to happen next. There was nothing to hold her back. Nothing was complicated, everything was new. She was falling in love with a great
guy. Everything else was a distant second—whether
she had chosen the right classes, how she was going
to cope with the very college-level amounts of work,
whether she'd get into the CNE dance company.

Ari remembered when she was falling in love with
Andy. When she wasn't with him, she'd been thinking
about him or dreaming of him. She'd felt giddy and
happy all the time. It had seemed as if nothing could
go wrong.

Now, it seemed as if everything had gone wrong.
And all because she'd fallen madly in love back in
high school. Ari headed toward the little hill at the far
end of the field.

Loren had predicted this, hadn't she? Ari thought.
She'd warned Ari, back before the accident. Back
when Ari's whole future was planned and perfect.
She'd warned Ari about going off to college with her
old boyfriend. In a strange way, what was happening
now was exactly what Loren had thought would happen. Old meant tied down. Old meant held back. Old
meant everyone else was out having new experiences
except you.

Silently, Ari crossed the big field. She tried to put
all thoughts out of her head, to make her mind a blank

and just feel the air on her face, hear the leaves rustling on the trees around the field, feel the way her footsteps pressed into the soft, grassy earth. It was so quiet back here, so peaceful. Ari took a deep breath, filling her lungs slowly and letting the breath out just as slowly. She felt some of the tension in her neck release.

Not too far away, someone was listening to music. Or playing the guitar. A fluid cadence of notes grew more pronounced as Ari got closer to the hill. She looked up. And felt her breath catch. Someone was sitting up at the top of the hill. Someone very familiar.

"Ben?" she called out.

The music stopped. "Ari?" he answered, a little uncertainly.

Ari jogged to the bottom of the hill and started to climb up quickly. She could feel her heart pounding out a drumroll, and it wasn't from the exertion. Of everyone in this whole big school, it was Ben at the top of this hill, Ari and Ben out here, just the two of them. Ari couldn't help but feel that it was fate.

"Hey! Of all people," Ben exclaimed. "You must have heard me thinking about you."

"You were thinking about me?" Ari felt her face grow warm in the cool night.

Ben nodded. "And here you are. Psychic connection, huh?" He played a few more notes and then put down his guitar. "Great spot," he said. "Good place to just get away." ·

Ari looked behind her and saw that it was. You could see most of the north campus spread out below, and in the distance were the dark silhouettes of mountains rising against the sky.

Ben patted the ground next to him. Ari sat down shyly. "So, what are you doing out my way?" he asked.

"Like you said, just getting away," Ari answered truthfully.

They sat for a while and didn't say anything. But it was a comfortable silence, a shared silence. Finally, Ben asked about the rest of her day. "Any reading lists as big as Greenburg's?"

"Not nearly," Ari said, "but there's still plenty of work in my other classes. Tomorrow, I've got my first Theater Improv class. We'll see how they manage to make homework for that. How about you? How'd your other classes go?"

"I only had one other one today. French Conversation. I always thought my French was pretty passable. We lived in France for a while, too, when I was little. I just wanted to brush up, get back what I used to know. But the teacher—"

"Don't tell me," Ari interrupted. "Could it be the famed Madame Duffy?"

"How did you know? Do you have her for something, too?"

Ari shook her head. "*Je ne parle pas français.* I took Spanish in high school. But let's just say Duffy's got a reputation."

Ben groaned. "I wish I'd known that when I was signing up for her class."

"Still time to switch," Ari said, borrowing Andy's line. It occurred to her that Andy could probably clue Ben in on what classes to take. *Ben, you ought to to talk to my boyfriend, the ghost. He's been auditing all kinds of classes.* Yeah, right.

Ari felt a tremor of discomfort. Ben, Andy. Andy, Ben. "Listen, I have to get going." She stood up and brushed some imaginary dirt from her jeans.

"You do?" Ben's voice made it clear that he wanted her to stay.

"Yeah. I need to, um, start some of that reading," Ari fibbed. "Let you get back to playing your music, being king of the hill up here."

"Well, if you have to. Hey, remember I told you tomorrow's my day to cook at the food co-op? I'd really like it if you'd be my guest."

Ari wanted badly to say yes. But she couldn't. What would she possibly tell Andy? "I'd like to, Ben. I really would. But I can't. Not tomorrow. I've got other plans."

"Oh." Ben didn't try to hide his disappointment. "Some other time, maybe?"

"Um, ah, let's see, okay?" Ari shifted from one foot to the other. All her tension had returned with a vengeance. "I've really got to run. It was nice bumping into you." She took off down the hill before Ben could say anything else.

Nice bumping into you. He must think I'm an idiot. Ari wanted to spin around and run back to him. Tell him that of course she'd come and try his homemade dinner. Tell him that she really didn't have to go back and study right now. Ask him his favorite color and his middle name . . .

But she held back. She had to hold back. Andy was with her because she'd said she needed him. Andy had saved her life. Arianne remembered the bone-chilling pull of the ocean, Andy's strong arms holding her, swimming for both of them. The way her terror had faded in his capable grasp. But he hadn't been strong enough to save her and himself as well. He had only enough strength to save one of them, and it had been Arianne.

Ari swallowed back hot tears. *I loved Andy. Correction. I love Andy.* Why was she thinking of him in the past when he was still very much in her present?

She heard Ben begin to strum his guitar again. She didn't turn around. But the sorrowful, bluesy tune followed her across the field. The truth of the matter was that she didn't want to go back to Andy right now. Ben's music beckoned her like a siren's song.

But she picked up speed and kept on walking until she couldn't hear the notes anymore.

sixteen

$\mathscr{D}$

$\mathscr{A}$*rianne dragged herself into the mail room. A boy* bounded past her, skipping down the three low steps to the room. People greeted one another energetically. They pulled envelopes out of mailboxes as if they were winning sweepstakes tickets. *Best years of your life.* That's what everyone kept saying college was supposed to be. And it looked to Ari as if it was true. For everyone but her.

It shouldn't have been this way. Ari's classes were excellent, tough but interesting. At least it seemed that way after her first few days. She loved her roommate. She had friends in the dorm. She'd had her first evening of work the other day, and it had been fine. All she had to do was collect people's CNE ID cards when they entered the gym, give them a towel, and hand back the ID cards when they left. Mostly, she could sit there and read and study. Or check out who had the funniest-looking ID picture when she got bored. But the best thing about it was that it provided a perfect excuse to get out of the room for the night, away from Andy and the tension swelling between them.

She scanned the rows and columns of mailboxes covering the wall nearest the door: 267, 286 . . . there it was, 278. She fiddled with the combination dial. She'd finally managed to get her combination memorized. She pulled open the box and a few colorful flyers slipped out—an announcement about who was playing at the coffeehouse next week, an invitation to a lecture about campus safety for new students. Farther back in the deep, narrow box was a slender, white envelope. She pulled it out and read the return address: "Loren Stephens, U Mass."

Arianne felt a minuscule lightening of her mood. Maybe a letter from Loren would cheer her up. She tore open the envelope. Loren's large, loopy writing covered a lined page torn out of a spiral-bound notebook.

Dear Ari,

Girlfriend, they oughtta let you sign up for Orientation Week all year long. It's really badly named, don't you think? When they send you the calendar for the school year, it should just say Par-TAY! on that first week.

Ari shook her head and laughed. This was just what the doctor ordered.

Hall parties, dorm parties, frat parties, breakfast, lunch and dinner parties, hanging out on the lawn parties, midnight parties in the TV lounge. My roommate, Sarah (she's really nice, except I don't know about her taste in music), says we're going to need a vacation before classes start (tomorrow, yeow!).

Ari turned over the envelope and glanced at the postmark. Right. Loren hadn't started classes when she'd written this letter. Probably wouldn't have made much difference if she had. Ari remembered Loren once telling her that academics were just a nasty side effect of school. She smiled as she continued reading.

And now for the really important stuff. Boys, boys, boys. Ari, they are everywhere. Cute ones, sexy ones, different than the ones I've been looking at for the past four years of my life. And let me tell you, I am one happy camper. There's this one guy, he lives up- stairs, I swear he looks just like Leonardo DiCaprio. (His name is John. Nothing so hip and exotic as our boy in Hollywood.) But he's pretty funny and we've been hanging out a little. There's another guy I like, too, George. He's a sophomore, but he got to campus early because he's on the basketball team and they've started practicing already. Tall, black guy with beau- tiful eyes and this totally incredible body.

John and George. Ari was sure there would be a Paul and a Ringo by the end of the semester. And a Pete and a Ned and a Steve . . .

And how about you, girl? Have you met any CNE cuties?

Ari thought of Ben. She couldn't help the way he just popped into her mind.

I hope so. I really hope you're having fun.

Suddenly, Loren's letter didn't seem quite so much like what the doctor ordered. Her words were a slap of unwelcome reality. Ari's spirits sank even lower as she finished the letter.

> And I hope you understand that I'm not saying I think you should be over Andy. We all loved him, Ari, and I know he's going to be a part of you forever. I just think it's probably really great for you to be starting someplace new, without all the built-in memories. Let that u-gly grin start happening again, girlfriend! (Kidding, kidding)

But instead of a grin, Ari felt a plump, hot tear roll down her cheek.

> Write and tell me all the news.
> Love ya,
> Loren

All the news. Sure. *Dear Loren, I unpacked my bags and you wouldn't believe who happened to pop out.* Ari couldn't imagine what she'd really write back to Loren.

"Bad news?" Ari looked up at the familiar voice. And there was Ben himself, live and in person, looking at her tear-streaked face with concern. Over the past few days, Ari mostly had kept her distance from him, sitting far away in Literature of Myth and just nodding a hello.

Now she wiped at her eyes with the back of her hand. "Not really." She shook her head and tried to smile. "Letter from my best friend from home. Actually, she's having a really great time at college."

Ben nodded slowly. "Uh-huh. And you're not? And that's the problem?"

Ari pressed her lips together miserably.

"I guess you have a pretty good reason. Ari, I heard the guy you were with died at the beginning of the summer."

Ari nodded. "No secrets around this joint, are there?" she said, hearing her voice come out small and wavery.

Ben shrugged. "Dorm life is like living in a small town. Anyway, I'm really sorry. It must be an awful thing to have to deal with."

"Thanks," Ari said softly.

"Is that why you didn't want to come to dinner the other night? Or is it me?"

Ari let out a noisy sigh. "No, it's not you. And yes, Andy's the reason why. I just—"

"You're having a hard time getting over him?" Ben supplied.

That was certainly one way of putting it, Ari thought. She simply nodded to Ben. What else could she do?

"Look, maybe it's none of my business, but it seems to me you've got to seize life. *Carpe diem.* Go out and live for both of you. Don't you think he'd want you to do that?"

Ari frowned. She couldn't tell Ben the truth, so why bother telling him anything at all?

"You know, Ari," he added gently, "you're not the one who died."

Ari felt a flash of anger. They'd spent one morning together and he thought he could tell her how to live her life. "You don't get it," she said tightly.

Ben shook his head. "Maybe I don't. But you could try telling me. I'd be happy to listen."

But Ari shut her mailbox forcefully, spun the combination dial, and started to walk away.

"Okay, don't tell me," she heard Ben call after her. "But if you change your mind, or just want some company, you know where I hang out."

Ari kept going. Why couldn't Ben just let her be miserable in peace?

"Why don't you come with us, Ari? Just for a change of scenery," Wendy invited. "We're going to hit the books for a while over at the library, and then we're going to stop at the student union and chill out."

Ari flopped down on her bed and shook her head. "I've got a lot of reading to do here," she said. "Besides, two's company."

"Three'll be company, too, I promise. We're going to study. We really are. And Mike said to invite you along. We won't do anything to embarrass you, I promise. No PDAs, no mushy stares. You've got my word, or I'll clean up the entire room by myself for the rest of the month."

Ari managed a laugh at that. "As if," she said. Wendy's dance clothes were draped over every available surface—chairs, her desk, her bed, the top of the bureau. Her half of the closet was nearly empty, but the floor was an obstacle course of shoes and clothes.

"Well, even if it was totally neat in here, you still need to get out of the room once in a while. I mean, you can't just sit around in the dark all the time. And if you're worried about being the third wheel, you could invite someone along, if you wanted." Wendy looked right at the begonia plant and frowned. "Gee, that's not doing too well, is it?"

Half the poor plant's leaves had turned yellow. The flowers were wilting. "I don't think the begonia's going to be with us much longer," Ari observed. "And P.S., I'm not inviting Ben out, okay?"

Wendy threw up her hands. "Just a suggestion."

"Well, I wish everyone would just stop suggesting things already!" Ari hadn't meant her voice to come out quite so harshly.

"Everyone? Well, excuse me," Wendy snapped back. "Okay, Ari, have it your way. Sit home alone every night. This 'everyone' isn't going to bug you anymore." Wendy went about gathering her books and papers silently, and left the room without another word. The door slammed behind her.

Anger raced through Ari's body. What business did Wendy have telling her how to spend her time? Why couldn't she sit here in the dark if she wanted? But then, there was a little voice of reason chasing the anger. Because Wendy didn't want to see her miserable, that's why.

Ari felt her throat get tight. This was the first fight she and Wendy had ever had. And the worst part was that Wendy was only trying to help. Wendy and Ben, too, Ari had to admit. It really had been the same thing in the mail room this morning. Ben had been trying to cheer her up. And Arianne had shut him down, just the way she'd shut down Wendy.

She felt awful. She knew she should apologize to both of them, but she wondered how she'd ever have the energy to do anything but lie here on her narrow bed. And where was Andy anyway? Here she was, cooped up in her room just to be with him and he was off the radar screen. "Andy? Hel-lo-o!" she called out to the ceiling.

The light suddenly shifted in the room. There was a pulse of brightness followed by a rapid-fire light-dark-light strobe effect. "Dum-dee-dee-dum!" she heard Andy's voice sing out. And then he was standing directly in front of her. "Honey! I'm ho-ome!"

Ari wasn't in the mood for Andy's jokes. She was about to ask where he'd been, but the dopey grin on his face told her he'd been hanging out with those doofs in the quad again. "Andy, can't you be serious for a minute?"

"Serious?" Andy twisted his face into a pronounced scowl. "Is this better?" Then he drew the corners of his mouth down even farther. He knit his eyebrows together until his eyes were crossed. He sucked in his cheeks until his face was a caricature. The effect was comic, but Ari didn't find herself wanting to laugh. He let his expression go back to normal. For a split second. Then he puffed out his cheeks and flared his nostrils and made his eyes huge. He seemed to be able to warp his features like Silly Putty. The third face did the trick. Ari felt her own mouth stretching into a little smile.

"Don't, Andy! Oh, my god, that one's awful."

"Made you laugh, made you laugh," he chanted. He sat down next to her on the bed.

"Andy?"

"Yeah, Ari?"

"We really have to talk. You know that."

Andy was quiet for a moment. He bit his lip. "Yeah. Okay."

"It's not the same anymore, is it?" Ari finally said.

"The same as what?" Andy wasn't making this easy.

"You know." Ari let her words hang in the air.

Andy didn't say anything for a long time. His comedy routine had given way to a genuine serious expression. Ari studied him—the chiseled planes of his face, his strong features, the lean, muscular lines of his body. She still found him incredibly handsome. He was the first boy she'd ever really loved. No one could ever be her first love again. But she couldn't keep going this way, and she didn't think Andy could either.

"So, what are we going to do, L.M.?" he finally asked. Ari noticed that his glowy form had faded to near transparent. He looked like a shadow next to her on the bed. She could see the telephone on the wall behind him, right through one of his arms.

She felt Andy slipping away from her. Again. A wave of undiluted despair crashed over her. In her mind, she was on the beach again, watching Jody's hopeless efforts to revive him. And there was nothing she could do to turn back the hands of time and do it all differently. Nothing at all.

"I don't know what we're going to do, Andy," she said. "I really don't."

seventeen
♨

"*You there! Dark hair, faraway eyes!*" Professor Greenburg barked. "What is it all these myths have in common?"

It took Ari a few seconds to realize he was talking to her, and she didn't have the vaguest idea what myths he was talking about. The blackboard was blank. No clue there. And she could feel her classmates staring at her, waiting for an answer. All she could do was study the graffiti on her desktop, her face burning with embarrassment. "I wasn't here," someone had scrawled stupidly. Ari could certainly relate.

Greenburg was so disgusted he didn't even grace her with one of his stinging barbs. He just turned away from her and moved on to the next person.

Ari tried to focus, but she could feel her thoughts drifting again. She looked toward the back of Ben's curly-haired head. He was sitting a safe distance away. He hadn't even looked at her as he'd come into class. Ari knew she wanted to apologize to him for yesterday. But past that, she wasn't sure about anything at all.

She felt as if she had swallowed a washing machine. Butterflies in her stomach just didn't describe the extent of it. She and Andy had kissed before she'd left for breakfast this morning, a deep, intense, passionate kiss. But the passion sprang from desperation, and they both knew it. She'd clung to him as if it might be the last kiss they'd share.

She didn't want him to go, but she didn't want him to stay. She thought about what Ben had said. About how she wasn't the one who had died. But she felt as if she wasn't really living, either. Which was Ben's point. Ari just hadn't wanted to admit it. He'd touched a raw nerve, and she'd howled. It was that simple.

Except that it wasn't simple at all. The bell peeled shrilly against all the metal and glass. Ari only wished she could be saved by the bell from her own thoughts.

Ben piled up his books and notebooks and stuffed his pen into the back pocket of his jeans. He studiously avoided turning around. Ari could feel it. She took a deep breath and headed toward him. Her heart beat quickly and nervously. "I'm sorry" was going to be the easy part. She had no idea what she'd say to him after that.

She intercepted him as he was halfway to the door. "Ben," she said. She could feel her voice tremble.

He stopped and looked at her. She couldn't read his face.

"Can I talk to you for a minute?"

"Sure," he said.

She trailed him out of the classroom. He stopped just outside the door. "Look, I wanted to apologize for the way I acted in the mail room yesterday," Ari said.

Ben nodded. He didn't say anything.

"I guess you just got kind of close to the truth," Ari admitted. "And it was hard for me to hear."

"Well, maybe I was a little out of line, too," Ben said coolly. "I don't know why I thought it was my place to go around holding any mirrors up. I mean, it's not like I really know you that well."

Oh, Ben, don't say that, Ari thought. Something had happened between them. They'd both felt it. They had a connection. Or at least they'd had one.

"I'm glad you said something," Ari told him. "I shouldn't have bitten your head off like that."

Ben put his hands on either side of his head and moved it from side to side. "Nope. Still here," he joked mildly. "Don't worry about it, okay?"

"Okay," said Ari.

"Well, see ya," he said. "Good luck with everything." He gave her a wan smile, turned, and walked down the hall.

Ari watched his back. This wasn't what she wanted to happen. "Do something, Ari!" she heard a voice deep inside her head.

Andy? She swiveled around, but he was nowhere. Couldn't be. She was imagining things. But Ben was really and truly walking away from her, heading for the stairwell, about to vanish. And she did want to do something. She ran after him.

"Ben!" she shouted. She knew people were turning to look at her. She sprinted and caught up to him at the top of the staircase. "Ben!" she said again. She put a hand on his arm.

He didn't move away. "Yeah?" he said.

"Um, well, yesterday you said that if I needed someone to talk to, you would listen." She looked up at him. His face was so near hers. His brown eyes had

138

amber flecks in them. There was a tiny scar over one eyebrow.

"Yeah, I did. I'm glad you asked."

Ari took a deep breath of relief. "Want to go sit outside or something?"

"Sure. You know, there's this interior courtyard in the art building. Beautiful little sculpture garden. We could hang out there, if you want."

"That sounds really nice." Ari was talking about more than just the garden.

A little gravel path wound through bold patches of brightly colored flowers and small trees. The sculptures were mostly modern, elegies to line and form in finely polished stone or cut steel, plastic, or wood sanded to a velvet finish. Ari and Ben sat on the stone bench at the center of the garden, watched over by an elongated, abstracted sculpture of a woman. The air was cool, but with the wings of the brick museum building all around them, and the open, sunny sky above, it was warmer in the courtyard than out on Central Bowl, more like spring than fall.

It was easy to talk to Ben there, too. Actually, it was easy to talk to Ben just about anywhere. "I guess I just can't bear to say good-bye to him," Ari told him.

"That sounds pretty normal to me," he said sympathetically.

"You think? I—I hear him sometimes," Ari admitted.

Ben didn't seem the least bit shocked. "You hear his voice? Yeah, I'd think that could happen. You hear something he might have said, a comment he might have made, a word of encouragement. You mean that kind of thing?''

"More or less," Ari said. "But Ben? I . . . see him, too.''

Ben arched a dark eyebrow at that one. ''Yeah?''

"I know. You must think I'm pretty crazy.''

"I think," said Ben, "that you must have really loved this guy a lot.''

"I did." Ari felt the sun on her face. "I do.''

"What was he like?" Ben asked.

Ari thought about Andy. The way he was before. She saw the two of them riding down one of the dirt fire roads on the ocean side of Portwater, the sweet smell of spring and sun on mud from the rain the night before. Andy cracking jokes as they rode. Trying to see who could make it to the next turn first. "Well," said Ari, "he was funny. A great athlete. Sweet. Stubborn, too.''

Ben rubbed her back lightly, briefly. "It must have been really awful for you when he died.''

Ari nodded. She swallowed hard. "Did you know that he died saving my life?''

The answer was all over Ben's shocked face. "Oh, wow, Ari. I didn't get that part of the story. That's really heavy.''

"Yeah," Ari said. They sat in silence for a minute or two.

"What happened?" Ben finally asked. "Or does it still hurt too much to talk about?''

Ari hadn't told anyone at CNE the whole story yet. Even Wendy had gotten just the bare facts: We got caught in a riptide; he tried to pull me to shore; I made it out; he didn't. Any more than that and Ari was battling the ocean again, swept out to sea on a current of terror.

140

But with Ben, it felt different. For the first time, she didn't feel herself shutting down. "It was right after graduation. We'd been out celebrating all night. We had this idea to go out to the beach and watch the sun rise."

"The sun rise? Oh, jeez, what an idiot I am!" Ben exclaimed.

Ari felt a beat of confusion. "You are?"

"Yeah. What was the first thing I ever asked you about? Your favorite time of day," Ben said. "And I told you mine was sunrise. Asked if you'd ever seen one." He shook his head. "No wonder you took off. But anyhow, I didn't mean to interrupt you."

"It's okay, and you're not an idiot," Ari said. "A bunch of us went down to the beach to watch the sun rise, and Andy and I decided to go swimming. It was a beautiful morning. The sky was bright pink at the horizon and just starting to get light. A few clouds, a little crescent moon still out. The ocean was strong. I could feel it as soon as I dove in. But it felt good that way, like it was going to wake us up. We started swimming out. We'd done it about a million times before. I mean, the ocean was kind of like our community pool. Most of my friends have been lifeguards at one point or another. We all grew up in the water . . ."

As she told the story, she was in two places at once. Back in the angry ocean, her mood going from elation to alarm, and here, in this sunny garden, safe with Ben. The sweet mildness of the air and Ben's open, reassuring expression were like an anchor. Her memories were powerful, but she knew she wasn't going to be carried away and swallowed by them.

She described the riptide, her realization that she couldn't get back to shore. Her panic as she watched

Andy swimming away without her. And her sense that the danger was over once she was in his strong hold. "He seemed so in control, I could feel him just churning through the current. The beach was getting closer. Our friends were there on shore. In my head, I was almost telling them about our narrow escape. You know, like, 'Whoa, we had some close call out there. You guys didn't see what was going on?' "

Ari paused. She felt a tightness in her chest. Ben just waited quietly. She rocked back and forth, ever so slightly. "Next thing I knew, we were buried under this huge wave, and then our friend Jody was pulling me out. But Andy . . . I didn't see him. And then Jody was dragging his body out of the water." She brushed hard at a stray tear. "One second I'm in his arms, and the next he's lying there on the wet sand. Except you could see that he wasn't there. It was really weird. I can't exactly explain it. His body was there, but you could just see that he wasn't in it. You know, like how you can feel when someone's in a room or standing behind you, even if you can't see him? Well, this was the opposite. I just knew he wasn't with us."

Ben nodded. Ari looked into his eyes. "He was gone." She felt the tears begin to flow, but she didn't try to stop them. "Because he'd turned back to save me. If he hadn't, he'd still be alive." She dropped her head and gave in to her sobs.

She felt Ben ease over and put his arm around her, his large hand on her shoulder. She leaned into him, the tears only coming faster and harder.

"Go ahead," he said, hugging her to him. "Let it all out. Yeah, that's right."

When she stopped, he let his hand slide down her arm, and he took her hand in his. There was no electric tingle, but his touch was wonderfully solid and steady. "So, you feel responsible for his death," Ben said gently. "That must be incredibly hard to live with."

"I am responsible."

Ben held her gaze in his. "Ari, he loved you. You can't go around feeling guilty about that."

"I owe him my life."

Andy put a warm palm on Ari's cheek. "You think he saved you so you could give up? Ari, what do you think Andy would want for you?"

"I think . . . he wants me to be happy." Ari felt the simple magic of Ben's substantial touch. Every nerve of her being felt tuned in to the place where his hand cupped her face. She felt as if she were falling into his gaze. She barely dared to breathe.

"Then you've got to do what makes you happy," he whispered.

It was the most natural thing in the world the way she turned her face up toward his and they drew nearer, nearer. His lips met hers. They were so soft and so gentle. The shared a tentative kiss, then drew back just enough to look at each other. She smiled. So did he. She wrapped her arms around him and drew him in for another kiss, a longer kiss, a deeper kiss. She could feel the lean muscles of his upper arms under her hands. She breathed in his scent. It had been a long time since she'd felt the pleasure of a palpable embrace.

Forgive me, Andy, she thought. She kissed Ben again. And again.

Ari stood outside the door to her room, her key in her hand. What if Andy was waiting for her in there? She put her ear close to the door and listened. No sound came from inside. She knew Wendy was out, because she'd just left her roomate at the dining hall after dinner, sitting around with Mike and Leslie and some of the others. But it didn't sound as if Andy was in, either. No bleeps and cries from Lost Treasure. No music on the radio. She felt a beat of relief.

But if Andy was out, it would only prolong what she had to do. Eventually, she was going to have to have a heart-to-heart with him, and it might as well be sooner rather than later.

Ari put her key in the door. How was she going to tell him? How was he going to take it? She never wanted to do anything to hurt Andy, ever. It had been the truth when she told Ben she loved Andy. But the kisses she and Ben had shared were the truth, too. She allowed herself a moment of instant replay—their lips together, their bodies close, his scent, the sound of their moist kisses, the sun pouring down on them in the little garden.

Ari sighed and turned the key in the lock. She pushed open the door. The first thing she noticed was the soft, flickering light in the room, as if it were lit by dozens of invisible candles. She heard the radio switch on. The first mellow notes of "If You Feel" filled the room. Their song. Ari's and Andy's song. And suddenly he was appearing right in front of her, and she felt the charge of his embrace as he took her in his arms.

She didn't have time to think. Out of habit, she felt herself responding to the music. Andy had always been a magnificent dancer—graceful, musical, sure in his movements. But now his step was even more ethereal. He led Ari lightly around the room. They hadn't slow danced together since graduation night. If only Ari could have banished every thought from her head, it would have been like dancing on their own little cloud.

But she didn't live on a cloud. She didn't want to be all alone on a cloud. Ari felt a tightness in her chest. Andy was being so romantic, so sweet and loving. How was she ever going to tell him the truth?

It was when he spun her around that she saw it. The begonia plant, sitting on the windowsill in a puddle of light. Somehow, with the dark of night already descended, a shaft of brilliant, golden daylight poured through the window. Every leaf on the plant was shiny green and vibrant. Tiny, fresh red flowers bloomed on every stem, and more buds were straining to burst open any second. The begonia had grown huge and beautiful in one day.

Ari felt herself gasp in amazement.

Andy stopped dancing and held Ari tenderly. "It just needed sunshine. That's all. It can't live in the shadows. And neither can you, L.M. Neither can you."

Ari looked up at Andy. Unshed tears gleamed in his eyes. She felt her heart opening up to him and threatening to break at the same time. "Andy . . ." She needed to say his name. "Andy, what will—"

"Shhh." He silenced her with a gentle kiss. "I don't know, but I can't live in the shadows, either." He stroked her hair and kissed the top of her head. "Good-bye, my Little Mermaid. Good-bye, Ari."

Suddenly, it was happening. Ari fought to keep from crying out for Andy to stay. She knew she had to let go. For both of them. "I love you," she said, her voice cracking. "I love you, Andy."

"Don't ever regret that, Ari. The better you love now, the more you'll be able to love again." She felt his electric kiss on her cheeks, her forehead, her eyes, mingling with her tears. "Eternally," he whispered, his gleaming form growing fainter, his voice sounding farther away. "Eternally yours."

He was going, going . . .

Arianne was alone.

Andy drifted in darkness. He'd left Ari's world behind. The lights of the CNE campus were no brighter or bigger than the faintest stars. Silence surrounded him. He let his focus wander, spread out, float farther up and away from where he'd been. He ambled in and out of conscious thought. He was in a twilight world, between wakefulness and sleep. All worries and pressures had faded away to nothing. But the pure bliss and dazzling light had not yet taken their hold.

Had he lost his way? Andy's concern about this was hazy. He no longer felt the sharp prod of time.

He could float here for a minute or forever; it made no difference. He made a loose, lazy bid at seeking out the radiant light. But he only encountered more of the void. Had he stayed too long where he didn't belong?

If he had, it had been worth it. His thoughts came together more concretely. Ari's tears had been different this time. He called up the beauty of her face, her dark, shining eyes. Those weren't tears of grief or rage or terror. Not anymore. He'd seen the loving memories in her gaze, felt her open to him and free him with her good-bye. He'd left Ari at peace, and he was at peace, too.

Andy felt himself swelling with love. Ari would be happy again, and he was happy, too. No regrets for her, and none for him, either. He felt a glint of gladness. This was enough for him.

And then the inky dark exploded around him. He was bathed in splendor and light and a deep, sheer joy. He let himself go with it, and the ecstasy spiraled.

The way was new, yet he was finally coming home to where he belonged.

nineteen

♒

Ari knocked softly on Ben's door. Then, a little louder. The problem was that everyone in their right mind was asleep. But she was giddy and excited, and she had her fingers crossed in a big way that Ben would want to be giddy and excited with her. She knocked again. How could she wake him without waking his roommate and everyone else on the hall? "Ben?" she called out in a stage whisper. She knocked once more. The third time was the charm. She heard a squeak of bedsprings and a shuffle of feet.

The door opened a crack, and Ben's head peeked out around it. His face was puffy with sleep. Only one eye was open. "Ari? My god, it's the middle of the night. Are you okay? Is something wrong?"

He looked so cute, all sleepy and rumpled. His curls stuck up at wild angles. "Everything's fine. Really fine, actually. Just don't hate me for waking you up. I'm going to watch the sun rise. I was hoping I could drag you out of bed to come with me."

Ben rubbed his eyes. "The sun rise?" A sleepy smile blossomed on his face. "Well, it looks like I'm up already, huh?"

Ari heard a groan from inside the room. "Ben?" a deep voice called. "What the heck's going on out there? It's the freakin' middle of the night, man."

Ben's head disappeared inside the room. "Go to sleep, Todd," Ari heard him say. "It's not time to get up yet." He looked back out at Ari. "Unless you're a little crazy," he added with a wink. "Wait right here, okay? Don't go anywhere." He fixed her with a look as if he might be dreaming and she might vanish.

"I'm not going anywhere," she assured him. "But hurry so we don't miss it." She felt an ear-to-ear grin stretch across her face as she waited in the empty hall.

The purple high-tops emerged first, sans feet, flung out of the room with a pair of socks. Ben emerged a minute later, hastily pulling on a pair of jeans, a sweatshirt held in the crook of his arm. Ari got a nice wake-up view of his thin but strong torso, his stomach muscles rippling as he pulled the sweatshirt over his head. He closed his door softly, sat down in the hall, and pulled on his socks and sneakers. One sock was red, the other black. The black one had a hole at the toe.

He stood up, and she noticed the toothbrush poking out of one front pocket. He took her hand. It felt every bit as wonderful as it had the day before. "C'mon," he said, his voice still rough with sleep. "Talk to me while I wash up. Otherwise, I might fall back asleep."

Ari let him lead her down the hall. "Wait, where are we going?" she asked as she saw where they were headed. "I can't go in there. See, it says 'Men.' "

"It does? Oh, is that what that word spells?" Ben didn't let go of her hand. He pulled her toward the bathroom. "Live dangerously, Ari. There won't be a soul in there, I promise. Just me and Tommy Tooth-brush.''

He pushed open the swinging door. Ari giggled and took one cautious step inside. A row of gleaming sinks with a long mirror that ran over them. Several toilet stalls on one side of the sinks. Two stall showers on the other. A couple of urinals on the wall opposite the sinks. That was the only difference. ''Oh,'' Ari said. She was a little disappointed. ''It's almost the same as ours.''

Ben laughed and squeezed a line of aqua toothpaste onto his brush. ''What'd you expect? You think we perform secret rituals in here?''

Ari watched him brush his teeth. ''Well, yeah, basically,'' she joked. She couldn't believe how comfortable she felt, standing here in the men's bathroom with Ben in the wee hours of the morning.

Ben gargled and rinsed. ''Well, yeah, basically we think that about you, too.'' They both laughed. ''In your case, of course, it's true. We see you female types go in there with your wands and brushes and secret ingredients and potions. Tools of the trade. Some of you even have little toolboxes full of stuff.''

''Vanity bags,'' Ari said.

''I'll say they are.'' Ben splashed some water on his face.

''No, I mean, that's what they're called. The toolboxes,'' Ari said, laughing. ''And you? You guys go in with a dirty towel. End of sentence. And for your information, *I* don't have a toolbox full of stuff.''

''You don't need it,'' Ben said seriously. He stopped what he was doing for a moment to look at her.

Ari smiled with happy embarrassment. ''That's sweet of you,'' she said.

She waited while Ben finished washing up. When he was done, he pushed open the bathroom door with his shoulder.

"Wait. Anyone out there?" Ari asked.

Ben made an overwrought gesture of looking down the hall, then an even more exaggerated gesture of looking the other way. Ari watched him hook his pinkies over his lower lip. She gave a start as he let out the top-volume, shrill whistle of a traffic cop. He waved her along with a melodramatic sweep of his arm.

Ari was laughing too hard to move. "Ben! All the sleeping beauties around here are going to kill you!"

"Then we'd better hurry up!" Ben grabbed her hand and they beat it out of the dorm. They only slowed when they got outside. "Oh, my god, are you nuts?" Ari laughed.

"Me? You're the one who got me up in the middle of the night."

It was still completely dark, except for the lights in the dorm. The grass was damp. The air was so cool Ari exhaled a plume of smoke. But her hand was warm in Ben's hand.

"Where to?" Ben asked. "Our hill?"

Ari felt a ripple of pleasure. *Our hill.* They had a place. "Our hill," she affirmed.

They started toward the gym and around to the field. "I'm glad you got me up," Ben said.

"Me, too."

"But, Ari?"

"Yeah?"

"Just don't try doing it every day, okay?" Ben stifled a little yawn.

"Deal," Ari said happily.

They crossed the field and climbed the hill, hand in hand the whole way. It was still inky dark when they got to the top. The campus was sleeping; the mountains, dark silhouettes. One lone truck made its way up the road to town.

"What are we going to do till the sun gets here?" Ben asked. He didn't wait for an answer. He just leaned in and kissed her.

Ari drank it in, responding with all her heart. They were still kissing as the first gray-pink light filtered through the darkness. They were still kissing when the sky around the hills blushed pink. They were still kissing as the horizon grew fiery.

Ben finally drew back slightly and looked around. "Almost," he said.

Ari looked around, too. The view was majestic and serene. Overhead, the sky was a deep blue, still studded with stars. As it came down to meet the earth, it changed, gradually, seamlessly, to lighter blue. Then to pink and orange behind the mountains and treetops, and the glowy undersides of a few wispy clouds.

Ari focused on the most intense area of color, a blaze of red and fuchsia and hot orange, over the mountains in the distance, behind campus. Suddenly a fire-orange splinter appeared at the edge of the silhouetted mountains. "Look!" Ari felt a rush of joy. The splinter swelled into a flattened dome. It grew plumper. Ari could feel Ben watching with her. A red circle of brilliance lifted up off the mountains.

Ari applauded. Ben joined in. They looked at each other, clapping and laughing. And then they were in each other's arms and they were kissing again.

It was a new day.

∂

In the Enchanted Hearts *series, romance with just a touch of magic makes for love stories that are a little more perfect than real life.*

In Cameron Dokey's Lost and Found, *the third title in the series, Amy Johnson is asked to use her clairvoyance to locate a kidnapping victim, the way she has in the past. Only this time it's not a stranger she must find—it's a guy she's met before—a guy she senses is her own true love.*

Lost and Found
𝒟

𝓗e was gone, and she would never find him again.

Amy Johnson sat at her bedroom window, her palms resting on the open sketchbook in her lap.

On the face she'd sketched just that morning. Hoping against hope that this time, it would be different. That this sketch would be the one to help her beat the odds she knew were stacked against her.

That it would be the one to help her call him back.

Usually, the view from her bedroom window was Amy's favorite thing in the whole world. But today, she hardly registered it.

She didn't notice the white sails of the boats skimming across sparkling blue water. The summer day's picture postcard perfection. Didn't see her own image, short brown hair, heart-shaped face, eyes the same color as the water, reflected in the windowpane.

Instead, her eyes saw what her mind saw. A thick gray emptiness. *Like the surface of the moon,* Amy thought. *Which is where I might as well be.*

She had to face the fact that she was never going to find him. The guy she'd met just once, but seemed unable to forget. The only guy who'd ever made her heart race, just with a smile. She could still remember the way surprise had lit his eyes when she'd smiled back.

But now he was two thousand miles away. Out of reach. And so was her best chance for true love.

"Amy?"

Amy started, her head jerking forward to crack against the window frame. With one hand, she reached to rub her smarting forehead. With the other, she quickly closed the sketchbook and thrust it behind the back cushion of the window seat.

She didn't want her father to see the sketchbook, or the portraits in it. She didn't want him to guess what she'd been doing. That she'd been trying to re-activate her talent, get it to work again. It would only worry him if he knew. And it would cause her mother to have an absolute fit.

Amy turned as she heard the door *snick* open. A moment later, her father's face peered around it. *Not quite in. Not quite out.* Amy thought with a flash of irritation. *The safe approach.*

"Dad," she said.

Even to her own ears, her voice sounded whiny. Amy hated it when she sounded like a baby. She could take care of herself, and she shouldn't have to keep on proving it.

"I thought we had an agreement," she went on, her tone more aggressive. "When my door is closed, you have to knock. You can't just barge right in. Now you've probably given me a black eye or something."

"I have been knocking, Amy," her father answered. He stepped all the way into the room but left the door ajar behind him.

"I knocked for a long time, in fact. Long enough for me to decide I'd better break our agreement to check and see if you were all right."

Amy felt a chill shoot through her.

It had been months since she'd heard her father use that careful tone of voice. Long enough so that she'd hoped the need for it had gone for good.

"I don't need you to check on me, Dad," she said, her voice sharp. "I'm not in here having a nervous breakdown."

Another one.

"I didn't say I thought you were," her father said.

Amy could feel his eyes on her. She looked up to meet them. They were the exact same color as her own. A vivid, multilayered blue. Deep ocean.

But there were dark shadows under her father's blue eyes. Shadows Amy knew she'd given him. Knew because they matched the ones she'd given herself.

Looking at her father's worried face, Amy felt her chill vanish as a wave of guilt washed over her.

Her parents had done everything they could to help her get over all the things that had happened last year in San Francisco. All the things that had finally been too much for her. They'd changed their whole lives.

Changed states, moving from California to Washington. Her mom had closed her thriving art gallery and was struggling to reestablish it. Her dad had gone from being a big-city detective to a small-town one.

Her parents had even waited to buy a new house until they'd found the perfect one for Amy, one where she could see the water from her bedroom window, because the water soothed her somehow. Made even the nightmares easier.

They'd given up everything. Torn apart their whole lives. All so Amy could have a chance to start again. To heal. And how was she paying them back? By being a jerk.

"I'm sorry, Dad," she got out, dismayed to find her voice choked with tears. "It's just—" Amy broke off, her throat too thick to continue.

It's just what? she thought. *It's just I was always so sure I'd be so happy if I woke up one morning to find that I could be the thing I'd always dreamed about but never was? Normal, not a freak. Not, "Oh, you're that Amy Johnson."*

Only now that I think it's finally happened, I can't handle it. Because it isn't what I really wanted after all?

Her father moved to sit beside her on the window seat. "Disturbance in the Force, huh?" he asked. Amy made a watery sound.

It was an old joke between them. Almost as old as their discovery of what they referred to as her talent. The thing that made her so different from everybody else. That had set her apart, even when she was small.

That had deprived her of childhood birthday parties, because the thing that she could do frightened the other kids' parents. Of dates when she'd grown older, because no guy wanted to go out with a girl who could read his mind.

It hadn't done any good to explain her talent didn't work that way. That she couldn't really read minds. Other people thought she could, and that was all that counted.

Except to her father, who'd told her she was like Luke Skywalker. That she was part of the Force. Her dad was the one who'd made her feel good about the strange thing she could do, Amy realized. The *only* one.

Amy was dismayed to feel her tears begin to slip silently down her cheeks.

"Hey now," her father said. "Take it easy, sport."

Amy reached up to wipe her wet cheeks. "Oh, Dad. I'm sorry."

"What's to be sorry about?" her father asked. "I've seen tears before. Manly men aren't afraid of a woman's tears," he continued, as if sharing secret knowledge.

He produced a large, white cotton handkerchief and held it up to Amy's face. "Here," he said. "Now blow."

Obediently, Amy blew her nose. She felt totally ridiculous, and incredibly better, all at the same time.

"I can do it myself, you know," she protested. "I'm not a baby."

"Are too," her father said.

"Am not."

"Booger face."

"Snot nose."

Amy could feel the grin starting to work its way from the corners of her mouth across the rest of her features.

She knew if she looked into her father's eyes the concern she'd shied away from earlier would be gone and they would be filled with laughter. She loved it when her father laughed. Hated it when he had to stop.

"Mucus man."

"Goober girl."

"Loogie Louic."

"Loogie *Louise*."

"Hey," Amy protested at once. "You stole mine. That's no fair. You can't do that."

"I'm your father," Stan Johnson answered. "I can do anything."

Impulsively, Amy threw her arms around his neck and buried her face against his shoulder. He'd made her feel better when she'd thought nothing could. He was right. He *could* do anything.

She felt her father's strong arms wrap around her holding her close. And safe. And warm. Just like always.

"So," Stan Johnson said softly, "you want to tell me what this is all about, sport?"

Oh, Dad, Amy thought. *I can't.*

She'd never told her parents about the one good thing that had happened those last days in California. A thing so unexpected, so remarkable and wonderful even in the midst of all the horror, Amy had almost begged her parents to give up their moving plans.

But how could she explain that she couldn't leave San Francisco—couldn't leave the scene of nightmares so vivid she woke up screaming—because moving to Washington meant she'd lose her only chance of being with a guy she'd met only once and might never see again?

A guy whose name she didn't even know, but whom Amy was absolutely positive was her true love. Her soul mate.

She couldn't. She couldn't even imagine attempting to explain that she'd fallen in love over something as simple as a conversation about ordinary things.

Other people had conversations like that all the time. Whether or not their sports teams had won. What their favorite flavor of ice cream was. But not Amy. Never Amy.

And then the chance meeting had ended as suddenly as it had started, shattered by the reality of her situation. She'd never told her parents about it, what it had meant to her to spend even a moment with someone who didn't know who she was, and so had

160

no expectations. None that didn't arise from what they could create together.

No, she'd never told her parents how much that simple thing had meant to her. And now, it was too late to say anything.

"No, I don't want to tell you what this is all about, sport," she answered.

Her father laughed under his breath, as if he wasn't quite ready to admit that she'd amused him.

Amy's mother hated her sarcasm. She called it an unhealthy defense mechanism. But it never seemed to bother her father. He always knew how to come right back. Her mom had also never agreed with Amy's decision to use her talent.

"Not the answer I was hoping for," Stan Johnson admitted now with a shake of his head. His blue eyes watched Amy for just a moment, as if trying to decide whether or not to push the issue. "But I guess it's one that I can live with."

Amy felt a surge of gratitude. Even when her father was worried, he trusted her. She sat up straight. Her father's arms fell away. But Amy swore she could still feel their support.

"I got Funny One out today."

Amy saw her father's eyes widen as they flickered over her shoulder to stare at the stuffed clown on her bed. Funny One.

"So you did," Stan Johnson commented.

The neutral voice was back in place again, Amy noted. But this time it didn't bother her. She could almost hear her father playing twenty questions inside his head.

Was the reappearance of Funny One a good development or a bad one? A move forward or a move back?

"He looks pretty good for an old guy."

"He's younger than you."

"Ouch," her father said.

Amy twisted around so that she, too, could look at the stuffed clown leaning up against her pillows. Over the years, his original vivid yellow-and-white coloring had faded to a uniform gray.

But Funny One was the only thing Amy had brought with her to her new home. The only memento she'd wanted from her past.

She'd kept him packed away until today, though. He had too many associations she wasn't sure she was ready to face. Because Funny One had been the start of everything. Holding him, the first proof that she was different.

Looking at him now, Amy felt something deep inside her shift. Felt her perception sharpen, as if some unseen hand had touched the knob which played back the images of the day and brought them into sudden focus. Perfect sense.

She saw again the boats on the water. Her own face reflected in the glass. And then a flash of light she hadn't registered before. Glancing from the windshield of the car she didn't recognize, backing out of her own driveway.

"There was someone here, wasn't there?" she asked. Behind her, she heard her father catch and hold his breath.

"I heard you and Mom talking to him, then you guys arguing. That's why I closed my door in the first place."

So she wouldn't have to hear the sound of her mother's voice. The panic in it. The anger and the pain. There was only thing that made her mother sound like that.

Fear. Fear for Amy.

"He was a cop, wasn't he?" Amy guessed. "But not from here. You didn't know him. He was a stranger."

At long last, she heard her father expel his pent-up breath. "He was from Seattle," he answered. "Something happened there today. Something like—"

He broke off, and Amy heard him rub his hand across his face. It made a scratchy sound, the way it usually did. Her father had a five o'clock shadow by ten in the morning.

And he always rubbed his face when he was thinking something he didn't quite know how to say.

But Amy knew what it was. Knew her father didn't need to say it.

"He wants to see me, doesn't he?" she said.

Jennifer Baker is the author of over thirty novels for young readers, a creator of original Web content and Web dramas, and the Director of Development for a major book packager. She lives in New York City with her husband and son.

GET READY FOR THE STORM...

AVONtempest

PRESENTS CONTEMPORARY FICTION
FOR TEENS

SMACK
by Melvin Burgess
73223-8/$6.99 US

LITTLE JORDAN
by Marly Youmans
73136-3/$6.99 US/$8.99 Can

ANOTHER KIND OF MONDAY
by William E. Coles Jr.
73133-9/$6.99 US/$8.99 Can

FADE FAR AWAY
by Francess Lantz
79372-5/$6.99 US/$8.99 Can

THE CHINA GARDEN
by Liz Berry
73228-9/$6.99 US/$8.99 Can